Once Upon a Christmastime

Cassie O'Brien & Raven McAllan

Lady Caroline's Unexpected Christmas Guest

Cassie O'Brien

Bertram, Marquis of Osborne, looked into the depths of his fast-emptying brandy glass and swirled the last dregs around the bowl with a frown. "Still, there's no escaping it, Piggy. Marry I must, even tho I don't wish it…and soon."

His companion, Percival Irving Gilliard, a vision of sartorial elegance, bore not the least resemblance to the nickname bestowed on him at school when the ten-year-old inmates boarding with him at Harrow had discovered the unfortunate arrangement of his initials.

Used now only by those who had become close friends from that time, Lord Percy, otherwise known as the Earl of Avondale, didn't flinch as he considered the matter. "Well, of this year's debutantes, I'd say Miss Emily Woodward and Miss Bella DeBurke are the best of the bunch, Bertie. Pretty girls, good figures. Neither of them look like they'd turn down the offer of a title. Or there's Miss Deveraux. In her second season but stunningly beautiful. She's obviously holding out for a good match."

3

The marquis' frown deepened. "There you have it. If I'm to marry against my inclination, I don't want it to be to someone who would turn my life upside down. These girls come with expectations. I'd have to do the pretty and dance attendance on them. They'd object if I spent too much time at my club or out with my rod and line. I'm damn comfortable with my life, and that's the way I want it to stay."

Sitting in a rather more than comfortable high-backed leather armchair in said gentleman's club, Percy crossed one immaculately clad leg over the other. "I suppose there's always Lady Mary. In her third season, she doesn't bother about anything much at all."

Bertie's chuckle rumbled up from the depths of his belly as befitted a man of bear-like proportions whose wild and somewhat shaggy looks his valet never quite managed to tame. "Including the bathtub. No, thanks. That's not what I meant when I said comfortable."

Percy gazed into space and swallowed his last mouthful of brandy. "You'd better take our Caro then. She does at least know where the bathing chamber is."

Bertie spluttered. "Caro? Your sister? I thought she was destined for the local bishop?"

Percy shrugged. "No. You'd have thought she'd be grateful for the offer after four failed Seasons, but she wouldn't take him. He didn't like the pups of the hounds well enough apparently, which is where she spends all her time when she ain't hogging the bathtub to wash the stink of the kennels off herself."

Bertie thought back and pictured Lady Caroline as he'd last seen her. Percy's trim figure was the epitome of masculine grace and always had been. His sister had been awkward to the point of clumsy, her cheeks blushing rosy with discomfort every time she stumbled, unable to control the cage of hoops and welter of material that comprised the Court dress of her crinoline. Then Queen Victoria had died, the following Season had been cancelled, and Caroline disappeared from Town never to be seen since. He'd felt sorry for her, although that didn't to give him the slightest urge to be saddled with her presence for the rest of his life. "Ah... Um..."

The hopeful look in Percy's eyes stopped him from saying more.

Percy sat straighter. "Come home with me tomorrow, Bertie? We have a big shoot on Christmas Eve to provide fowl for the feast. You'll enjoy that."

There was nothing better looming on the horizon for the twelve days of Christmas, and he acknowledged to himself Percy knew that fact as well. Bertie was an orphan with no siblings, and it was only the entail on the Estate that obliged him to marry before he reached the arbitrary age of thirty-five. He glanced heavenward, searching for a suitable excuse, but none came to him to permit his turning down an invitation from such a long-standing friend. *Damn! But what can it hurt? I'll give her no encouragement and if I know anything about the matter, she'll be more than happy with that arrangement, too.*

"I'd be delighted, of course."

Percy beckoned the waiter to bring the decanter and refill their glasses. "Excellent. I'll call for you in my motor carriage around midday? My man doubles as chauffeur, and yours can take the boot seat."

Bertie forced a smile to his lips. "I'll look forward to it." *Or the fowl shoot at least.*

Lady Caroline sank down and rested her neck on the back of the bathtub with a sigh as hot water caressed her skin. After a day of physical exertion, the luxury provided by the house's recent installation of a heated plumbing system was utter bliss. The soap smelt of violets. She passed it over her body, creamy with foaming bubbles. This was the life, now her mother had given up on her matchmaking endeavours. Why Mama had thought she would be happy to be at the beck and call of a man just for the privilege of wearing a gold wedding band was beyond stupid, and the crocodile tears her mother had shed at her rejection of the only marriage proposal she'd ever received moved Caroline not one jot.

A thick fluffy towel awaited when she pulled the plug and stepped out of the tub. Water gurgled, and she watched it disappear with a sense of wonder for the minds behind the modern innovation which provided such convenience. No more lugging buckets of water up and down the back stairs for the servants, and no more carrying open chamber pots through the house — Avondale Manor now possessed several lavatories with a running water flush, and even the staff quarters had been supplied with one.

The tub emptied, Caroline draped the towel over its edge, donned a belted dressing gown, and walked to her bedroom.

Her maid, Jenny, opened the wardrobe door when she stepped over the threshold. "Have you company at dinner tonight, my lady? Shall I lay out your velvet skirt?"

Caroline shrugged. "Not as such. Reverend Taylor and his curate will be in attendance, along with the Misses Hayward from the Parish Council. My navy-blue surge will suffice."

Jenny smiled. "To make arrangements for the wassail to call? You'll like that."

Her mistress returned her smile two-fold. "Yes, I will. I've consulted Cook, and each child is to receive a sweet, sticky gingerbread man with a silver thruppenny bit for his middle button from the tree. Their parents may take home any of the fowl not required for the house after the shoot."

"You are ever generous to the village children at Christmas, my lady."

Caroline dispensed with her dressing gown and stepped into her drawers. "I would wish they could keep a farthing or two back to buy a stick of toffee from the shop, but I fear it will not be so."

"Begging your pardon, my lady, but none will be worse off for that," Jenny replied stoutly as she fastened the silky Directoire knickers around her mistress' waist. "Each child will have their Christmas treat, and the family will find comfort in having a little extra coinage to help feed them during the barren months until spring. Will you wear an evening blouse or…?"

Caroline shook her head. "No. It's not necessary. A camisole under one of fine lawn, with perhaps a collar and cuffs of lace."

Her requirements met and her dark-blonde hair dressed in a simple plaited coronet, she surveyed her reflection, turning back and forth in front of a full-length mirror. Neat, with no requirement to have a padded bustle strapped to her backside when in the country, the fashionable slim-line silhouette of the Edwardian era flattered her figure as the balloon-shaped Victoriana gowns of her youth had not. The wretched things had swamped her form and made her appear nearly as wide as she was tall.

The mantel clock struck the dinner hour of five. Early hours were kept in the country, especially during the winter months. The sound startled Caroline. "Goodness! I must go down. Mama will have been entertaining our guests for at least fifteen minutes on her own, and you know she dislikes having to do so."

Jenny handed her a lace-edged handkerchief. "If I know anything about the matter, the clergy along with the Misses Hayward will be sat in the drawing room entertaining themselves at present. It has come to my ears the dowager has taken to instructing her maid to listen for your door to open and close before she herself descends."

"Oh dear. Well, at least the reverend is a good man who will not take offence at being left unwelcomed by an absence of his hosts."

Jenny nodded. "And from that circumstance the other guests will take their lead, I'm sure."

Caroline agreed and left the room, making sure she closed the door behind her with a suitably audible snap. The previously damp and chilly hallway was agreeably warm with the addition of the new cast-iron hot water-filled radiators set along its length. Gas lamps set on the wood-panelled walls provided more illumination than candle sconces ever had. All in all, what had been a hurried scuttle towards the roaring log fires that heated the public rooms downstairs was now a pleasant saunter without the need for a shawl—but as she neared the head of the stairs, the racket of a commotion assailed her ears.

Too noisy for the arrival of the reverend's party. Caroline hurried forward, only to halt in her tracks when she saw her brother, and more particularly, who also stood in the vestibule. *Please… Not him…* The heat of a crimson blush rose on her cheeks. *Not without notice to prepare…*

Pride and several years of maturity since she had last caught sight of Lord Osborne came to her rescue. She took a deep breath in and thought of happier things, which calmed her agitation and enabled her to walk down the stairs without her cheeks looking like a couple of ripe tomatoes. "You're home early, Percy. We weren't expecting you for another two days yet."

Percy was lord of the manor in his rightful place as head of the family, and the slight note of censure in his sister's voice for his inconsideration was not noticed. He handed his cane and hat to the butler with a shrug. "Change of plans, Caro. Bertie was at a loose end, so here we are, ready to join the festivities."

She bit her lip to prevent herself from smiling at the knowledge of the 'festive fun' that was coming his way that evening. "How lovely. I'm sure Reverend Taylor will be delighted to see you, as will the Misses Hayward."

Percy's jaw dropped. "What? The reverend and the local tabbies? Caro, you could have warned me."

Caroline gave him her sweetest smile. "Deary me. If only you'd sent a telegram to say you were arriving home earlier than planned, I could have rearranged the occasion to become luncheon tomorrow from which you could have excused yourself to attend to Estate business. Still, our guests are already with us, so chop-chop, Percy. I'll put dinner back until six to give yourself and Lord Osborne half an hour to freshen up."

She would have liked a few moments to collect her thoughts again before facing their unexpected visitor, but polite etiquette dictated she greet him without undue hesitation, as it also ensured that having returned home to find guests in his house, Percy had no choice but to take his place at the dinner table.

Her heart hammered against her ribs as she did so. "Lord Osborne, welcome. We would be happy to see you at dinner, but if the exertions of your travel have fatigued you, say the word and a tray will be sent to your room."

His smile was as infectious as she'd always found it. A gleam lit his eye as if he fully appreciated the by-play between herself and Percy. Her knees trembled just for being near him. *Tarnation!* Her girlish crush was as intoxicating to her senses as he ever had been in London.

Good grief, she's changed somewhat…

The words ran through Bertie's mind as he met Lady Caroline's green-eyed gaze, although fortunately they were not what came out of his mouth. "I'm delighted to see you again. It's been quite some while since we last met." He paused, waiting expectantly for her to hold out her hand with fingers extended or curled to indicate her preference to receive a shake or a brief kiss on the back of it.

She did neither but kept her arms at her sides. "Indeed, it has."

Which was odd, until he noticed her gaze was fixed at a point over his shoulder. She gave an imperceptible nod to the unseen rustle of a female dress behind him, and he realised her attention was being required in two places at once. Good. That must mean the lamps had been lit, the curtains drawn, and sheets applied to the bed in whichever guest room he had been assigned.

Lady Caroline returned her attention to his face. "Johnstone will show you up. The tray?"

He appreciated her gesture in offering him an excuse not to attend a dinner Percy was so patently not looking forward to, but with the perfect manners of a man who knew his duty as a house guest, he turned it down with self-depreciating smile. "I thank you, but a journey of only a few hours is not enough to tire a man of

13

my proportions. I would like to join the dinner table if my unexpected appearance will not discomfort the guests already invited?"

"They will be honoured, I'm…"

Her sentence was not to be finished as the dowager appeared on the staircase, her face wreathed in smiles. "Percy, my darling, *darling* boy, you're home." She clasped his hands in hers when she reached him. "Did you sense how much I wished for it to be so? You must have, for here you are."

"I am, Mama. And I've brought a companion with me to attend the shoot."

Lady Caroline beckoned the butler forward then excused herself to attend to her other guests. Neither her brother nor her mother noticed her departure.

Percy led the dowager closer. "You remember Lord Osborne, don't you, Mama?"

She held out her hand. "I do. Your journey passed tolerably, I hope? Percy's Daimler motor carriage possesses a high degree of comfort, I believe."

Bertie took his cue and brushed his lips across the back of it. "Perfect luxury. The miles raced by in a flash."

She looked pleased at his complimenting it. "You may take me in."

Percy objected. "We can't sit to table in our dirt, Mama. You must excuse us for a few minutes."

She looked them up and down. "It's only the reverend. He won't mind."

Percy leaned forward and whispered a word in her ear. Bertie couldn't make out what it was, but it seemed to do the trick.

"Yes… Well… Of course… Come down to the drawing room when you're ready." She turned away.

Johnstone stepped forward, and Bertie asked as they followed the butler up the stairs, "And the magic word was?"

Percy winked, mouthed the word *lavatory*, and both of them grinned.

The sanctuary of his guest room was soon gained, and inside it, Bertie found his valet, Ridgley, unpacking his luggage. A small log burned in the grate, cheerful but giving out little heat—that seemed to be the job of a rectangular arrangement of cast-iron tubes attached to the wall under the window.

It gurgled, and his valet tutted. "It's been doing that at intervals, my lord. I hope it doesn't keep it up all night or you'll hardly get a wink of sleep."

Bertie examined it. "There appears to be a tap thing on the end of it. I think it can be turned off."

"I shall make sure to do so when I bring up your nightcap. Will you require your evening wear? Tie and tails."

"No. Dinner is informal this evening. A clean shirt and a wash will suffice."

Ridgley did his best to tidy him up, and Bertie contemplated the alteration in Percy's sister while his valet did so. Lady Caroline had been gauche, clumsy, and awkward when she arrived in the capital for her first Season at seventeen, and several more after it had done nothing to improve her self-assurance, but now…

Ridgley smoothed Bertie's jacket over his shoulders to remove any hint of wrinkle. He thanked him, descended the stairs, and quirked an eyebrow at the footman sitting on the chair beside the front door. The servant jumped to attention as people tended to do when Bertie sent an enquiring glance in their direction.

"The drawing room is this way, your lordship."

Bertie followed him and made sure to acknowledge the man's service, knowing his large frame could be intimidating to those of smaller stature. The footman opened the door. He stepped into the room and paused at the sight of

Lady Caroline, her eyes sparkling and her face animated as she spoke.

"I will have decorated the Christmas tree that afternoon, and before the children sing, the footmen will light the candles on it and Johnstone will turn down the gas lamps…"

She's really quite pretty. How didn't I realise?

She clapped her hands together. "It will be magical."

Ranged in front of her, sitting on a sofa and two armchairs, two men and two women appeared equally delighted.

The dowager didn't look similarly enamoured, although her expression brightened at his entering the room. "Lord Osborne, you are suitably refreshed, I hope?"

"I thank you, I am."

The two men stood.

Lady Caroline's expression froze. She gazed intently at the floor, then turned her head towards him. It was such a brief hesitation he wouldn't have caught it if she hadn't been in his direct eyeline.

The excitement dissipated from her face, and she made an introduction of each guest in turn. "The Reverend Taylor, his curate, Mr Wells, Miss Maria Hayward, and her sister, Miss Edith."

He gave a half bow to each of the ladies, offered the men his hand to shake, and completed the formalities by kissing the back of the dowager's hand. Lady Caroline's lay unoffered in her lap. On a whim, he reached for it and pulled it to his lips. The jolt that raced through him matched the surprise in her eyes. She snatched her hand away, but that didn't stop a certain part of his anatomy from twitching expectantly in the trouser department.

Drat the man! Why did he do that?

Caroline's cheeks burned. She refocused her gaze on the floor. *Think of the puppies. Think of the puppies. Think of the puppies...*

An image of Goldie and Serpia chasing their tails around and around provided her salvation, and the heat on her face faded. Percy sauntering into the room gave her the final diversion she needed to regain a more serene composure.

Her mother jumped to her feet. "*Darling*, are you ravenous? You must be, I'm sure. Shall we adjourn and eat our dinner?"

Her brother cast a longing glance at the sherry decanter. "Yes, Mama, of course. My apologies for being tardy. I've kept you waiting."

"Not at all, darling. I'm sure I won't mind if my soup is a *little* cold."

Percy took the hint and offered his mother his arm. Lord Osborne did the same to her, which she resolutely pretended not to see and instead linked her arms, one through each of the Misses Hayward.

Lord Osborne took his rejection gracefully and followed along behind them in the company of the clergy—while she ground her teeth at the ease at which he conversed with people he'd only just been introduced to. The details of the wassail were his before they reached the breakfast parlour, which was used for other meals besides where the number of those eating would be lost in the far grander space of the formal dining room with its table that could comfortably seat forty.

The table in the parlour was round. Percy took his place, Mama to his left and Lord Osborne next to her. According to protocol, Caroline should have taken the chair to her brother's right, but only one thought ran through her head. *Far too close for comfort.* So, she thumbed her nose at that particular rule of etiquette, left the place vacant for one of the Misses Hayward, and sat two places farther away in between the chairs destined for the Reverend Taylor and his curate, Mr Wells.

Reverend Taylor intoned grace, then as both he and his curate were hearty trenchermen, Caroline was not obliged to provide much in the way of polite conversation apart from acknowledging their compliments as they worked their way through the courses that included a large joint of roasted beef sirloin accompanied by rich gravy and batter puddings. Talking across the table was still frowned on by her mother unless they were dining *en famille*, leaving her free to concentrate on her plate while listening to other conversations taking place without any obligation to join in.

Mama was entertaining Lord Osborne with the detail of the far grander affair that was to take place on Christmas night—an occasion Caroline fully intended to be indisposed for, as she was every time Lady Penelope Stamford's name appeared on the guest list. Penelope was of a similar age. Her cruel jibes had the ability to turn Caroline's face cherry-red at the drop of a hat and had been the bane of her childhood, and of the Seasons in Town that followed it. Percy was regarding Miss Maria with a glazed expression as she relayed her recent adventures with the vagaries of the church organ, and she was pleased to see Lord Osborne include Miss Edith in his conversation with her mama by way of a kind remark or two.

The plates of the final course were cleared to be replaced with a decanter of port, a stilton cheese, and a bowl of assorted nuts—the sign for the ladies to withdraw.

Reverend Taylor glanced at his pocket watch. "My goodness, how time has flown. We must leave you or I will sleep through the call to Matins."

A young man, full of zesty ardour for his newfound calling, his curate jumped to his feet, his face aghast at the prospect of Lauds being left unsaid.

The reverend looked at the Misses Hayward. "If we may offer you a ride home, my dears? We came in the pony and trap."

They accepted happily, and Percy's face immediately brightened. "Do you fancy a frame or two of billiards before bed, Bertie? I've some fine cigars in the humidor."

That offer accepted, the dowager rang the bell and summoned Johnstone. Caroline pre-empted any further attempt at blush-inducing social niceties while farewells and goodnights were exchanged by slipping her hands under her thighs and sitting on them.

She was last to leave the parlour and padded silently up the stairs to her room. She found sleep evaded her, though, when she slipped beneath the bedcovers. *Drat the man for disturbing her peace again*! The mound between her legs throbbed. Her nipples hardened. Living in the country with a predilection for striding the fields on foot and with free access to an ample library, she was not at all ignorant of what her body was yearning for as many gently bred unmarried females might be. She longed for his touch, for them to be naked together, skin on skin, and to have his hardness assuage the burning need of the secret, wet place between her legs.

Double drat! It wasn't only that her face had the potential to betray her when Lord Osborne was nearby, but her body, too. She would forgo a visit to the breakfast parlour in the morning. An extra hour in the kennels would hopefully restore her equilibrium.

Three large brandies and half a dozen frames later, Bertie felt sleepy enough to bid Percy goodnight and retire to bed. Ridgley was in his dressing room, an iron filled with hot coals in his hand as he attended to any garment that had become creased from being packed into his travelling trunk. He set it aside and dealt with Bertie's discarded clothing while he undressed. His nightshirt and dressing gown donned, he wandered into the bedroom in search of a book while Ridgley slipped downstairs to fetch his nightcap—a mug of bitter cocoa to which a generous tot of rum had been added.

A small selection of volumes were displayed on a shelf fixed to the wall to the left of the desk, and on inspection, he picked a leather-bound copy of short stories featuring the detective Holmes, and his sidekick, Watson. A comfortable armchair and convenient side table had been provided. Bertie settled down to read until his hot drink arrived but soon found the words of Conan Doyle not holding his attention as they normally did. His mind seemed determined to wander, and in only one direction: Lady Caroline. He tried once more to absorb the words on the page, then gave up the attempt and let his thoughts roam where they would.

He hadn't done her justice when he'd seen her in the drawing room earlier, he decided. Her face wasn't just *quite* pretty, but remarkably so—its delicate bone structure accentuated by an upswept hairstyle rather than being hidden by the drooping bunches of ringlets that had dangled to each side of it during her Seasons in London. Her figure and form had become elegant, but it was something more than those newly revealed attributes that fascinated him. There was something about her that raised his protective hackles as he also wished to be one of the people who could put the sparkle in her eyes and set free her laugh.

His cocoa arrived, and he resolved to be up and about early the following morning to attend breakfast downstairs rather than request Ridgley to bring it to his room on a tray as had been his original intention.

His efforts were not rewarded. Only Percy was at the breakfast table, and he apologised.

"Forgive me, Bertie? I've been buttonholed by the Estate's land agent. There are some matters needing my attention. The trout lake is well-stocked, though? If you'd care to cast a line or two?"

Bertie tucked into his kedgeree and accepted, more than happy with an offer that allowed him to indulge in his preferred sport. "I would, thank you."

He never travelled without the equipment and clothing necessary to participate in his pastime and an hour later descended the main staircase clad in a waxed jacket, sturdy gaiter boots, and his battered old felt trilby to which his flies and lures were attached. His ensemble was completed by a creel in one hand and several rod bags in the other. Lady Caroline was crossing the hall when he reached the bottom of the flight, and he paused to wish her good morning.

Many a lady hostess of his acquaintance would have looked slightly askance at the sight of one of her house guests loping off to pursue a solitary pursuit rather than being available to attend the luncheon, picnic, recital, or whatever she had planned. Lady Caroline obviously didn't mind one bit. In fact, Bertie thought her face seemed somewhat relieved as she glanced at the creel and rods in his hands.

"Off fishing, Lord Osborne?"

He smiled and tried to lessen the formality between them. "Your brother has invited me to try my luck at the trout lake. May we use first names between ourselves? Call me Bertie, as he does?"

Her expression appeared uncertain for a moment, but then she nodded and crunched down on the apple she was holding. He took in her outfit. An ankle-length skirt made of dark gaberdine, a no-nonsense white blouse, and a serge jacket that pinched her waist and ended at her hips. Practical outdoor clothing for sure.

From what Percy had told him, he took a guess while shifting his creel and rods into one hand so as to be able to open the front door.

"You're going to the kennels? I'd like to see the hounds, if I may?"

She thrust her hands, half-eaten apple and all, deep into her skirt pockets. "Ah… I'd best not detain you from your sport. The dogs won't have been released into their compound as yet. Perhaps you would care to call in on your way back to the house when the kennels will be…shall we say…slightly more fragrant?"

Bertie chuckled. "I'll admit it's not a scent I'm particularly partial to, so thank you for warning me, and I'll do as you suggest."

She smiled back at him, then preceded him through the door.

A gamekeeper waited for him outside. Bertie handed him half his tackle and asked as Caroline walked on, "What will I find in the lake? Brown trout? Rainbow?"

The man shouldered his burden. "Mainly brown, but you'll find none the worse sport for that, my lord. Cunning little sods, they are. They'll resist your lures and line if they can."

Bertie found his prediction to be accurate and was pleased by the time the afternoon light was beginning to fade to have landed several plump specimens. The smaller fry he threw back before picking up the creel containing his catch. He gave it to the gamekeeper to deliver to the kitchens, then the man showed him the way to the kennels which seemed to be contained in a substantial barn.

As he approached, lamplight spilled out of the open door, and the noise was terrific—a cacophony of barking mixed with excited high-pitched yelps. The reason for it became obvious when he looked through the door. Around the perimeter the space was sub-divided into kennel houses. Two lads were visiting each in turn and depositing large bowls of meat and kitchen scraps. The residents all appeared to be working dogs, but gun and sheep rather than fox hunting hounds, and the remainder of the floor space, which was the majority of it, was laid out like a show jumping arena, although canine not equestrian.

A complicated agility course had been set up, and he watched Caroline test two golden retrievers over it, her lithe figure running beside them using only hand signals to command. He couldn't keep the admiration from his voice when they completed the task and he called to her, "Oh, well done. That was marvellous."

She turned in his direction and smiled. "Hello, Bertie. You found us then?"

His heart double tapped, and he felt as if the sun had just come out on a rainy day. The dogs nosed her skirt, and she caressed the scruff under their chins, while Bertie's beard practically quivered its demand for her fingers do the same to him.

He walked closer. "That I did. Who are these handsome pair?"

She clicked her fingers above the head of the nearest dog. It reared to its hind legs and danced in a circle. "This is Bella." She repeated the sequence with the other. "And Honey."

Both dogs received a treat from her pocket when they regained all four legs. She asked a kennel lad to bed them down for the night. Bertie picked up his rods at the door and accompanied her back to the house. The December air noticeably colder with the waning of the day, she pulled her sleeves down over her hands and enquired about his catch. He asked how long it had taken her to train Bella and Honey and would have asked more had the house taken longer to reach.

"Sit beside me at dinner? I'd like to know about the different hand signals."

That seemed to give her pause just when he thought she was feeling more at ease in his company.

"Ah…"

He plastered his best attempt at a soulful, hound-dog expression onto his face. "To save me from a fate worse than death?"

Her mouth twitched. "Such as?"

"The placement of the table on Christmas night. The dances that will follow. The suitability of the supper menu for those evening guests not attending the dinner. The…"

Caroline's eyes lit up, and she giggled. "Say no more. I will come to your rescue."

Bertie was delighted to hear her do so and chuckled. "Then I will meet you in the drawing room at the appointed hour with every expectation of relishing my dinner rather than wishing it was over and done with."

Caroline mounted the stairs, her heart thumping. From the warmth in his eyes, it seemed Bertie actually liked her. She could nearly think he was paying her the type of attention that indicated he was interested in knowing her better. Or was she reading too much into it? Was he just being kind? She conceded that was the more likely case, but even so, she was pleased with herself as nothing she had said or done had given her true feelings away.

The bathing chamber nearest to her bedroom was directly opposite it. It had once been one of the smaller guest rooms, several of which had been converted to accommodate the new plumbing arrangements. She stopped by, put the plug into its appointed hole, and set the tub to fill. Jenny assisted her out of her day clothes and into her dressing gown, then she soaked in the hot scented water for the best part of half an hour.

She pictured Bertie's face, the plump lips she would like to kiss, the soft beard she longed to stroke. The hot water lapping over her breasts made her aware of her nakedness. She wondered what Bertie would look like similarly unclothed in the tub, and her mound throbbed. *Too much.* She needed to regain her composure before dinner, so sat straighter and pulled out the plug— but still a spark of hope must have remained, for she found herself asking Jenny for her midnight-blue velvet skirt and a lace evening blouse that didn't button all the way up to the neck.

The dinner guests were to be the local squire and his wife, along with Lady Penelope's parents, the Right Honourable Richard Budleigh-Benson and Mrs Edith Budleigh-Benson—although thankfully, not their now married daughter— plus a young baronet accompanied by his bride of six months. Only Bertie, sitting sipping from a glass, was in the drawing room when she entered it.

He smiled and stood. "You look lovely, Caro. May I pour you a sherry, or must we wait until Johnstone returns to perform the honours?"

She swallowed hard. *Bertie thinks I look nice.* The blood rushed to her cheeks, and she stared at the floor. *Think of the puppies. Think of the puppies. Think of the puppies.* The heat faded as she did. "Thank you. If you're happy to pour it?"

He handed it to her, and Mama and Percy walked into the room. Johnstone ushered the remainder of the guests in five minutes later and resumed his sherry distribution duties. Caroline's serenity returned while she sipped, and with a mischievous wink, Bertie topped her glass up again when no one was paying attention.

Dinner was announced, and Bertie stood behind his chair looking expectantly at the one beside it and only took his own place after she sat on it. Wine was poured, and dinner passed in a haze of enjoyment. They talked of dogs and fishing, and the one dish she actually remembered eating by the end of it was the second course—freshly filleted brown trout, pan fried with lemon and capers.

She left the table with the rest of the ladies as the final course was cleared, leaving the males to empty the port decanter and enjoy their blue-veined cheese. Tea would be served in the drawing room while they waited for the men to join them, but in the midst of the rustle of skirts making their way to it, she overheard Mrs Budleigh-Benson wittering on to her mother of how excited *'darling Penelope was to be returning home for Christmas for the first time since she'd wed dear Sir Walter'* and decided in the interest of self-preservation it was time to retire to her room.

She hesitated when the newly married bride exclaimed excitedly, "Lord Percy has promised to show us his new wind-up gramophone when the gentlemen return to the drawing room. He has three discs to play on it, he said."

Like her brother, Caroline adored his latest acquisition of a machine that miraculously poured music out of its trumpet-shaped horn, so was tempted to remain. But the prospect of listening to Penelope's doting mother extolling her daughter's virtues for the next hour or so was just too awful to contemplate, so she bid her mama goodnight and beat a hasty retreat up the stairs.

She entered her bedroom, looked at the timepiece on the mantel and found it to be not quite ten o'clock. A little early to be sleeping, but tomorrow was Christmas Eve. One of her favourite days of the year and also one of the busiest. The novel she was halfway through was on the night table beside her bed, but she didn't pick it up and instead asked Jenny to turn off the gas lamps. The room darkened, and she fell asleep wondering if Bertie was enjoying hearing the music played on the gramophone and whether he might be just a little bit disappointed at not finding her in the drawing room.

In the morning, she was up and dressed shortly after dawn. Her first port of call was the kitchen, and she took with her a small pouch of silver coins and a reel of red satin ribbon to give to Mrs Wright, the cook. The rooms that comprised the below-stairs work engine of the house were bustling. Servants bobbed or bowed and stood to one side as she walked through. She acknowledged them all by name with a cheery, "Good morning!"

There were twenty children living in the village of a suitable age to receive a gingerbread man, and Caroline counted the thruppenny pieces out, deciding twenty-five should be made in lieu of any family having a small Christmas visitor in tow. The silver coin would be added to the shape before it was baked, the red ribbon threaded through its head while the biscuit was still warm, and the final detail piped onto it in white icing once it had cooled and hardened.

Next, Caroline made her way to the kennels. The sky had lightened considerably but was overcast, although with no heavy rain-laden clouds, which boded well for the shoot.

Stimpson, the kennel manager, thought so, too. "They'll be no squinting into the sun for the sportsmen at the pegs today, I'm thinking, my lady."

She agreed. "Or much prospect of a drenching. The birds will stand out beautifully on such a grey day once the beaters have got them in flight."

The gun dogs selected to be part of the drive and subsequent recovery of the game were milling around in the central floor space of the barn. Partridge, pheasant, and pigeon should be plentiful, and the beaters would also work the tall rushes around the edge of the lake to entice wild ducks and geese to break cover. In the soft mouths of the retrievers and spaniels, the dead game birds would be returned to the shooter, then the whole process would begin again with a new drive over fresh ground.

Caroline pursed her lips and whistled a two-note call. The dogs bounced up to her, yipping, their tails wagging. Seven golden retrievers for the heavier birds, and four spaniels to bring home the partridge and pigeon. Two clicks of her tongue accompanied by half a dozen hand signals had them all lined up in order of size in front of her. She bent and ran her hands over the body of each dog then surveyed their lips for any abrasion that would preclude their taking part in the day's sport. Satisfied, she straightened and listened to a babble of male voices becoming louder—the sportsmen had arrived.

She nodded her approval for the condition of the dogs to Stimpson, then snapped her fingers to summon her favourite retriever to her side. Bonnie pranced up to her skirt. She bade her "Heel," and walked to the barn door with the dog following in close order. A head and shoulders above the rest, Bertie was unmistakable among the men approaching the building.

She fixed her eye on him, pointed, and gave Bonnie the command, "Seek. Stay. Fetch." Bonnie streaked away, bounded up to Bertie, and settled to trot one pace behind him, her nose level with his knee.

The dog understood her message. Would he?

Bertie's face registered surprise, then he looked up and tipped his hat in her direction. She smiled and stepped into the shadows of the barn. A door in the far corner of it allowed her to return to the house without having to mingle with those gathering at the double-width doors to the front of it.

The manor was even more of a hive of activity when she returned. Male servants lugged the trunks of those guests who had arrived during her absence to their rooms. Housemaids scurried back and forth delivering refreshments to where they were needed. A groundsman and two under-gardeners were manhandling a potted nine-foot spruce tree into position beside the grand staircase while four excited tweenie maids hovered beside boxes containing ribbons, small candles, and glass baubles to dress it. The smell of Christmas greenery was divine. Caroline smiled to all and sundry until a voice she loathed spoke from above her.

"Oh, look, Mama. The tree is in place. I must run down at once and give my advice to the maids."

A complacent voice answered, "They will appreciate it, I'm sure. No one has an eye for fine detail like you do, Penelope."

Dread settled over Caroline. Her blood seemed to freeze in her veins. *Oh, good God, what's she doing here already? I was sure Mama said Christmas Day not Christmas Eve.*

She must have misheard but at least she hadn't yet been spotted, so with her footfall soft and silent, Caroline stepped backwards, pushed open the green baize door leading to the rearstairs, and faded from sight.

Bertie counted his contribution to the Christmas feast with satisfaction and looked forward to thanking Caroline for loaning him Bonnie whose mouth hadn't damaged so much as a single feather so far as he could see. He handed his beater, loader, and pick-up boy a generous tip and walked back to the house with the men who had comprised the gun party. They were all in as high grig as he was himself, and congratulations along with hip flasks were passed around.

A soak in the tub before dinner beckoned, and the first thing Bertie saw as he entered the house was a magnificent Christmas tree, its branches decorated with tiny candles in silver holders, red ribbons, and an assortment hand-painted glass baubles. A silver star adorned the apex, but as he mounted the staircase, he realised what he hadn't seen were any gingerbread men dangling from the branches. *Ah well, perhaps they can only be added at the last minute.*

Ridgley awaited him in his room. He selected a tailed evening jacket and held it up for his master's approval. "I have been informed there are additional guests sitting to dinner this evening, my lord. And although not as many as are promised for tomorrow, the state dining room is being used tonight. The meal will be served somewhat later than previously. The gong will sound at eight."

Bertie nodded his agreement that the occasion warranted formal wear. "Black tie then, not white."

Ridgley bowed. "Of course, my lord."

Bertie found the tub in the bathing chamber satisfactorily generous, and while he was too large to recline in it, he didn't have to bend his knees to become level with his chest as was so often the case. On the night he had arrived, the reverend had imparted that the wassail called at the house in the early evening around six, and eager to see the pleasure on Caroline's face when it did, he chivvied Ridgley to work fast. Thankfully, if his valet thought it strange his master wished to be ready a full two hours ahead of dinner, there was nothing in his demeanour that showed it.

Percy and his mama were in the drawing room when he entered it, as were the older couple, Mr and Mrs Budleigh-Benson he'd met the previous night. With them was a gentleman of similar age to their own accompanied by a younger brunette-haired lady he vaguely recognised, although not from where.

Piggy looked up as he closed the door. "Evening, Bertie. No need to stand on ceremony. The sherry and glasses are on the sideboard."

Bertie gave a half-bow to the room then availed himself of the offer.

Percy completed the social formalities by naming the remaining guests. "I think you may remember Lady Penelope, or Miss Budleigh-Benson as she was when she and Caro enjoyed their Seasons in London? Sir Walter Stanhope is the lucky man who won her hand."

Her face fell into place. He remembered her being at one or two of the same soirees as Caroline. Bertie nodded and smiled politely in her direction then shook her husband's proffered hand.

They seemed a mismatched pairing. Sir Walter portly and ruddy of face. Lady Penelope, considerably more youthful, and with a deep cleavage her husband seemed to glance at with proprietary pride.

The dowager waved her hand at the Budleigh-Bensons and explained matters further. "Richard and Edith are our nearest neighbours and my dearest friends. I like to think Penelope is as much at home here as she is anywhere."

Lady Penelope kissed her fingers to her. "By your kindness, yes, I am."

A tap sounded on the door, and it swung open to reveal a housemaid carrying a tray laden with gingerbread men. She bent her knee and bobbed to the dowager. "Beggin' your pardon, ma'am. Mrs Wright says as these are finished and ready for Lady Caroline to hang on the tree."

Lady Penelope walked closer and surveyed the tray. "You may pass our thanks on to Cook. They are delightful. Follow me, and I will oversee their arrangement."

Bertie looked at Piggy. "Ah…should that task not wait? Your sister's not here yet."

With a sway of her hips, Lady Penelope sauntered past him. "Oh, Caroline won't mind. She'd be the first to tell you my artistry is superior to hers."

The dowager smiled fondly. "Dear Penelope is practically one of the family. She and Caro spent many hours together here when they were young. Before my darling Edward passed and Penelope married Sir Walter."

If that was supposed to resolve the matter, it didn't and left Bertie feeling uneasy. Where was the consideration for Caroline in all of this? If he knew how she felt about the wassail, why didn't her mother and brother? Why did they allow her to be dismissed so easily?

It was not his place to object, though, and he sipped his sherry while watching the beribboned biscuits being added to the tree through the open door. The room filled, and he glanced at every new arrival, but Caroline had still not appeared when Johnstone ushered the carollers into the hall.

Glasses were refilled, and the company watched the village singers assemble in front of the Christmas tree. Bertie set down his glass and walked into the hall itself. Surely Caroline would appear to hand out the treats she had so carefully prepared?

The reverend called the adult choir to order, and they sang *God Rest Ye Merry Gentlemen* with gusto, followed by an equally enthusiastic rendition of *Hark the Herald Angels Sing*. Mugs of warm mulled wine were passed to them by the maids, and the children lined up. A movement caught Bertie's eye in the far corner of the hall as the candles were lit and the gas lights turned down. The green baize door leading to the servant's domain swung open a few inches, although nobody came through it.

He saw Miss Emily Hayward must have noticed it, too. The children began to sing *Silent Night* in clear piping voices, and she oh-so-casually drifted towards the door, then her lips moved as if she were speaking to someone concealed behind it.

The carol finished, and Lady Penelope practically ran out of the drawing room. "Come, come, gather around. I have a little something for you all on the tree."

The children clustered around her, and she plucked the gingerbread men from the branches and passed them to outstretched hands. The green baize door closed. Miss Emily moved back to join her sister. Bertie glanced left then right. Lady Penelope had stepped seamlessly into Caroline's shoes, and apparently not one person apart from him had even noticed the exchange. Something was out of kilter. He resolved to have a discreet word with one or both of the Misses Hayward if an opportunity arose.

Caroline was glad she'd risked taking a peek at the children and made her way down the backstairs to the kitchen to thank Mrs Wright for producing the gingerbread men. She felt a pang of regret she wasn't able to join in the festivities, but that was more than offset by the relief of not being obliged to attend an event now guaranteed to set her nerves on edge by the early arrival of her nemesis.

Mrs Wright's face reflected her pleasure at being praised for her efforts. Caroline gave her leave to distribute any remaining gingerbread men between the tweenie maids, then requested her supper to be bought to the library on a tray. Well used to this request during a house party, Mrs Wright assured her it would be with her shortly.

Caroline thanked her then entered the realm of the servants' domain to reach her destination. None who saw her so much as blinked. They were used to seeing her there. The narrow back passages behind the green baize doors had provided her with an escape route to get away from Penelope since she had first discovered their existence as a child.

She took the key from the library door and slipped it into her pocket. Another legacy from Penelope, who had thought it amusing to shove her into a small cobwebby cupboard when she was four and lock it. It had taken several terrifying hours in the darkness with spiders, real or imagined, crawling over her skin before her location had been discovered. Penelope had, as usual, assumed an air of innocent concern at how such an accident could have happened, and since then Caroline had never willingly entered any room where she could be trapped in solitary confinement.

As promised, her supper was not long in arriving. She laid down the periodical she was reading and relished the bowl of hot oxtail soup along with the rabbit pie that accompanied it. A rosewood occasional table was home to brandy and whisky decanters. She poured a generous measure of the latter and sipped it, reading until her eyelids felt suitably heavy.

She exited the room. Raucous laughter assailed her ears and, fleet of foot, she raced up the backstairs and entered the refuge of her bedroom. The mantel clock struck twelve. She closed the door, wished Jenny a heartfelt Happy Christmas, and gave her a golden guinea along with a leave of absence so she could spend the holiday with her family. Jenny expressed her doubts over her mistress' ability to dress herself as she did every

44

Christmas Eve, which, as usual, made Caroline smile as she shooed her out of the door.

The peel of church bells ringing celebratory rounds woke her in the morning. She swung her legs out of bed, opened the curtains, and threw open the window. A hard frost had settled overnight, leaving the air coldly crystalline. The low sun would climb and melt the icy particles by mid-morning, but to greet the day the landscape was coated in white—pristine and sparkling.

Her nose became numb, and Caroline shut the window then dressed in a skirt that fastened at the side and a button-fronted blouse. Her boots presented more of a problem. The art of using the button hook required to fasten them was beyond her skill, but a pair of lace-up leather pumps she more normally wore in summer provided the solution. Her hair she brushed and pinned into a simple bun on the nape of her neck.

The click of doors opening or closing sounded outside her room—house guests used the bathrooms then made their way downstairs to enjoy a festive breakfast. She waited until the noise quietened then used the back passages to leave the house. To do so involved walking through the kitchen, and she pinched a freshly grilled sausage from Cook's skillet and wrapped it in a hunk of bread. She exchanged Christmas wishes with all the staff she met along the way and dabbed her lips on her handkerchief once she finished eating.

She reached the kennels. The dogs were yapping or yelping in expectation of their morning exercise, and she whistled to call her pack to her. A five-mile hike over hard ground satisfied them but left Caroline's feet absolutely frozen in her thin-soled shoes, and she was more than happy to return to the barn. She asked one of the kennel lads to bring her a cup of tea from the kettle that sat atop the pot-bellied stove heating the barn, then sat on the straw-strewn floor to pet and play with her dogs until it arrived. She was halfway through planning an agility course for them when her thoughts were interrupted, and it was not by the delivery of her drink.

"Happy Christmas, Caro."

She looked up and silently pleaded with her face not to give her away. "And Happy Christmas to you, too, Bertie."

He walked closer, and Bonnie, recognising his scent, trotted to him and nosed his trousered knee. He hunkered down to pet her with no regard to the prospect of dirtying his Harris tweed suit and scratched the place between her ears no dog could reach for themselves. Bonnie panted with pleasure, her tongue lolling, and he smiled.

"Good girl. Can you smell I have a reward for you in my pocket, if your mistress says you may have it?"

He glanced at her. She nodded her permission. He produced a linen handkerchief and unfolded it to display a grilled bacon chop that an hour or so previously would have been on the breakfast table. Caroline pulled a handful of broken biscuits from her pocket and distracted the remainder of the pack while Bonnie, her tail wagging at double speed, gobbled up her treat.

Bertie straightened. "I missed your company at dinner last evening as maybe the children did earlier?"

Caroline, while naming no names, felt relaxed enough surrounded by her hounds to be somewhat candid in her reply. "We had some early arrivals yesterday. Too many for my peace of mind, I'm afraid."

"So, you asked Lady Penelope to give the children their Christmas gift in your place?"

She couldn't help but laugh a little at that assumption. "Ah…not exactly. Penelope adores to be in the limelight. She would have taken the task for herself even had I been present. I did see the happiness on their faces, though, which to me, was the point."

"From behind the green door?"

Caroline answered with a smile for him having noticed, but Bertie frowned. "You arranged the treat, yet it was not even so much as acknowledged that the gift was from you. That doesn't seem right to me."

Naturally timid from childhood, that she was often 'out of sight, out of mind', and lonely due to her inability to mingle, she was not prepared to admit. The chance that the look in Bertie's eyes would change from *like* to *feeling sorry for* was a risk too far. She had said enough so closed the subject down and diverted the conversation towards a less personal path.

"It was by my choice, Bertie. No one barred me from joining the wassail except myself. Are you playing in Percy's annual billiards tournament after luncheon?"

Happily, Bertie followed her lead, took out his pocket watch, and looked at the time. "I am and should return to the house. The lottery to decide the pairings takes place shortly."

Caroline smiled. "I wish you the good fortune of obtaining a skilful partner when the names are pulled. Percy says there are a couple of real old duffers taking part. He fears for the baize every time one of them picks up a cue."

He chuckled as he left her. "I will hope luck is on my side then."

Bertie walked away from the barn, admiring Caroline's stance while not altogether agreeing with it. To his mind, Lady Penelope had overstepped the mark—her attitude high-handed and presumptuous—and he found the dowager's easy acceptance of it even odder than he had before. His opinion of Lady Penelope did not improve at luncheon. She arrived at the table and sat in Caroline's allocated place on Percy's right without so much as a backward glance, for all the world as if she were the daughter of the house. Bertie ate to the accompaniment of an exhibition of liveliness guaranteed to turn heads in her direction. By the end of the meal, her incessant chatter was getting on his nerves, as were her frequent outbursts of throaty laughter, and he was more than grateful to see the dessert course cleared.

The ladies retired to the drawing room to make up their fours and play bridge. The men made their way to the billiard table where fat cigars were lit and glasses of claret or brandy passed around. Thankfully, the two duffers decided to withdraw from the lists in favour of spending more time with the decanters, and Bertie, ably partnered by Sir Alexander Brand, acquitted himself well, finishing in second place, beaten by Percy and Viscount Wilfred Woodruff.

Only an hour remained until dinner would be served once the tournament was complete. Bertie hastened to his room to change his day suit for evening wear and made it down to the drawing room ten minutes before the gong. All signs of the card tables had disappeared, and the furniture had been moved to leave more floor space for guests to stand and chat. He took a glass from the footman's tray and moved deeper into the room.

Percy appeared at his shoulder and nudged his arm. "Penelope was in the dining room as I walked past it. Moving place cards. I slipped in after she left. She's seated herself beside you."

Bertie glanced casually in her direction. Her low-cut evening gown of gold-coloured satin was so perfectly moulded to her form it bore all the signs of having been created by a first-class modiste and must have cost Sir Walter a pretty penny. She was in the midst of a chattering group and seemed as likely to give him earache as she had at luncheon.

He returned his attention to Percy who leaned a little closer and lowered his voice. "Your luck might be in. Penelope likes to indulge herself once in a while now she's provided the heir and spare. Sir Walter's quite a tippler as you saw this afternoon. He won't notice if she slips upstairs with you for an hour or so, and if he does, I'll head him off until you both reappear."

Bertie took another quick look. Her wasp-waist and uplifted breasts showed her corsetry to be as expensive as her dress. A few years previously, he may have been interested enough to return to his room and place his sheep-gut sheath into a dish of water to become useably pliable, but the appeal of such scrambled encounters had long since faded. When he made love to a lady, it was a leisurely affair to be savoured, and preferably with a mistress who knew the rules of engagement. His last arrangement had ended by mutual consent two months previously when the Duke of Northdean had offered the lady concerned twice as much for her annual expenses—a price Bertie had not been willing to match, and with Caroline occupying his thoughts, nor was it a vacancy he had any interest in filling.

He asked Percy to return the favour. "Not for me, I'm afraid. Go check your decanters and move her along a few places?"

Percy agreed then admitted, "Or me neither. The old boy in the trousers just isn't interested in someone I've known since she was a snotty-nosed brat."

Bertie sipped his sherry while he was gone and passed a few pleasantries with Sir John Bletchley whom he also knew from his club while half hoping Caroline would have a change of heart and put in an appearance. He was still doing so as dinner was announced.

He took his place at the table and found Percy had done him proud. To one side his dinner companion was a middle-aged widow who'd definitely imbibed more than one sherry and had several amusing stories to tell. On the other, an equally good-natured young matron. The Christmas feast was everything that had been promised. The game birds had been cooked to perfection, the sides and sauces were delicious, and the wine an excellent vintage.

The men did not linger over their port and joined the ladies in the ballroom after only one glass. Musicians were tuning their instruments as additional guests arrived, and it was at that point Bertie's evening began to go downhill. He accepted a glass of champagne offered on a tray, and Lady Penelope materialised at his side. As manners dictated, he gave her the glass then took another.

She sipped and peeked flirtatiously up at him from beneath lowered lashes. "Naughty of me, I know, but I hoped to sit next to you at dinner. I changed my place card, but Mr Whitby-Smyth must have wished for my company, too, for I found I was seated next to him."

The next move should have been for Bertie to have exclaimed how much he would have enjoyed to have her sitting by him while initiating contact by patting her hand, which she would have then laid on his arm. He didn't oblige.

"I'm sure Mr Whitby-Smyth was suitably entertained. Indeed, I see him glancing in your direction."

She didn't take the hint but pouted and leaned in closer to give him a better view of her decolletage rising like two full moons from the low-cut bodice of her gown. "He's a rather a bore, actually. Not at all the type of company I'm looking for. It takes a big man to satisfy me. Someone like…"

She ran the tip of tongue provocatively over her top lip and left her sentence unfinished, although she might just as well have added the 'you', such was the lascivious speculation in her eyes. Bertie sensed trouble. Lady Penelope either didn't know the rules of engagement or chose not to abide by them. He hadn't, however, reached the age of thirty-three without learning how to excuse himself where a situation called for it and managed to palm her off on a passing baronet in order to fulfil his duty as a single male house guest and mark his name on the dance cards of both the Misses Hayward and the merry widow.

His breathing space lasted less than half an hour. The band struck up a lively poker, and he led Miss Emily onto the floor. Lady Penelope and the baronet slid in beside them, and she was one step behind him throughout the dance, then the waltz, and again for the valse. During the next dance, she stumbled close by him and lurched into his arms. Too much of a gentleman to let her fall, Bertie caught her then stood her back on her feet, his patience wearing thin.

A break from the festivities was most certainly required, and he left the ballroom to recover his good humour by way of a brandy in the billiards room—a male preserve that even the most determined of females wouldn't dream of entering. A slither of light shone under the library door when he passed it and, on impulse, he detoured into it in search of a periodical to take with him. The sight that greeted him when he shut the door behind him restored the smile to his face.

Caroline, snug in a loose robe of cherry velvet belted at the waist, relaxed on a cushioned sofa with her legs tucked up beside her. Standing on a rosewood table in front of the sofa was a plate containing several sandwiches—ham, he thought, a wedge of cheese, and an apple. Beside it a cut-glass crystal tumbler was half-full of what appeared to be neat whisky. The matching decanter was also present.

She looked up from her book as the door latch clicked shut and offered him a key she took from her pocket. "Lock it, Bertie? If there's any possibility another guest may take to wandering around the house in search of where you've got to."

He did so with alacrity and moved closer. "Is that Scotch?"

She nodded and gestured towards a side cabinet. "There's a glass in there if you want a tot."

He very much did, so fetched one and poured himself a healthy slug. The fiery liquid warmed the back of his throat, and he sniffed the peaty tones emanating from the glass appreciatively.

Caroline's voice was amused. "Are you going to stand there and just knock it back or take a seat and tell me what has sent you from the party post haste in dire need of a large whisky?"

Bertie nudged an armchair closer to her sofa and sat. "I'm getting past enjoying these type of house parties. I think you've got the better idea. Supper, a nip of something nice, a good book, and no requirement to be polite to people you don't much care for."

She laid her book down on the table. "I won't put you on the spot and enquire as to any names, but I take it one or more of our guests has ruffled your feathers?"

With a strong inkling that although she'd not admitted any such thing, Caroline shared his opinion of Lady Penelope, he swirled his drink around his glass and answered, "The same person who also ruffles yours, I believe?"

She took his meaning immediately. "What did she do?"

He summed it up in three words. "Tiresome, pushy, persistent."

Caroline toasted him with her glass. "You forgot spoiled, precious, and sneaky."

Bertie chuckled. "I thought our viewpoints may coincide. What were you reading before I disturbed you?"

She handed him a slim volume published by the *Daily Mail* to commemorate the achievement of Louis Bleriot in winning their one thousand pound prize when he became the first person to cross the English Channel by means of powered flight in July. "You're interested in air travel, Caro?"

Enthusiasm lit her face. "I adore the thought of being able to soar into the sky. Did you enjoy Percy's gramophone? I long to drive his motor carriage, but he won't teach me. It's not very ladylike, he says."

Bertie's heart thumped. Delight fizzled through his veins. She was pretty, enjoyed country pursuits, and now this. *Perfect.*

"Then I'll teach you, if you like?"

"Percy won't lend you his Daimler for that."

Bertie grinned. "No, but he will lend me his Daimler to take you for a drive and won't know who's behind the wheel once we're out of sight."

Caroline sat straighter and clapped her hands together. "Oh, yes please. When?"

The urge to kiss her was nearly overwhelming, but it was too soon, so he kept his seat and smiled. "Tomorrow. After luncheon."

He knew his heart belonged to her when she enthusiastically accepted, then cocked her head to one side and said, "I don't suppose you play cribbage or chess, do you?"

Caroline sat before her mirror for Jenny to brush and dress her hair, her face reflecting her pleasurable anticipation at the day that was to come. Never had she felt so happy. Over the past five days she and Bertie had fallen into a wonderful routine. She spent the mornings with her dogs, he with his rods, and when the rest of those staying at the house assembled for luncheon, they drove off in the Daimler with a picnic basket on the back seat.

To her delight, she found she possessed a natural aptitude to steer and control the vehicle after an initial burst of bumpy stops and starts as she mastered the timing of gear changes and foot pedals. They'd so far visited several local beauty spots and the day previously had driven to the nearby city of Bristol and purchased a new glass disc of ragtime tunes to play on Percy's gramophone. Bertie had carried the machine into the library while the rest of the household were at dinner, and they enjoyed the music while eating the supper Bertie had taken to joining her for every evening since he'd discovered her habitual bolthole on Christmas night. Knowing him better hadn't in any way lessened her desire for him, and she fell asleep every night imagining his strong arms around her, his lips on hers, but with every passing day their newfound familiarity made her feelings easier to hide.

Jenny laying the hairbrush down on the dressing table pulled her from her reverie. "Are you quite well, my lady? You seem somewhat distracted."

Caroline smiled. "I was woolgathering, I'm afraid."

She stood and shrugged on the jacket Jenny held out for her then walked to the bedroom door. It seemed suitably quiet beyond it, so she turned the handle and prepared to make a quick dash along the hallway to the green door that lay in the opposite direction to the grand staircase. The hallway, however, wasn't quite empty, and her feet weren't quite fleet enough.

"Well, well, little mouse. Here you are at last."

Caroline's hands trembled, and she dug her fingernails into her palms. *Think of the puppies. Think of the puppies.* She squared her shoulders and tried for an air of dignity as she continued walking towards the green door. Lady Penelope's mocking tones followed her through it.

"That's right. Escape into your rat-run like the snivelling rodent you are…"

The door swung shut, cutting off any further insults, and Caroline breathed a sigh of relief. Penelope wouldn't follow. She would find no servant willing to show her the way through their domain. Penelope had always been careful not to be nasty to her where she might be seen or overheard by any other, but that didn't include the servants who she considered beneath her notice. They had witnessed Penelope's attacks, both verbal and physical, over the years. Several more deep breaths steadied Caroline's jangled nerves and enabled to make her way through the kitchen and out to the kennels, showing no outward sign of distress.

She crossed the yard and noticed the change in the weather. The air felt heavy. Thick black clouds gathered ominously above. If the sky fulfilled its promise, the hard-packed earth of the dirt tracks they drove on would become a sticky mud bath, and the motor vehicle would be going nowhere today. She entered the barn to the first splatters of rain and dispatched the kennel lads to give the dogs a short run before the weather worsened while she set out an agility course.

Bertie entered the kennels not five minutes later. She smiled. He didn't, and walked closer, concern etched on his face. He looked into her eyes when he reached her. "I heard her, Caro. I couldn't believe my ears. How long has she been bullying you like that?"

She gave him a rueful half-smile and shrugged. "Always."

He opened his arms, and without hesitation, she moved into them and tilted her face towards his. He put his mouth on hers, warm and sweet, and it felt entirely natural to part her lips. His tongue sought hers and hers his, their mouths fitting together like two halves of a peach, and her chest heaved as they broke apart.

He held her close. "Marry me, Caro? Please?"

Happiness and delight flooded through her. *Did I hear him right? Marriage. A wedding? Oh God, a wedding. Mama.* Panic set in as the reality of what that would involve dawned. She buried her face in his neck. "I can't."

Bertie held her tighter. "Why not, my love? I think you want to."

Her voice was muffled. "I do."

He tipped her chin upwards, gazed into her eyes, and her fears poured out of her mouth all in a rush.

"The wedding. Mama will insist on a full church. She'll invite half the county. I know it. They'll be no stopping her. Everyone will look at me as Percy escorts me up the aisle. And when they do my face will turn beet-red, and thinking of puppies won't be enough to stop it. The congregation will stare and laugh behind their hands at me. Then at you for choosing such an ugly bride, while speculating what could have befallen you to force you to do so." She buried her face in his neck once more. "I won't turn you into a laughing-stock, Bertie. I couldn't bear it."

Bertie held her tight to his chest and kissed the top of her head. His instinct was to dismiss those who would dare to be so crass as unimportant nobodies and, feeling Caroline tremble in his arms, damned Lady Penelope and all of her ilk to Dante's everlasting inferno. He thought he could persuade her, but why should he? The thought of his bride enduring what to her would be a day of torment was not the way he wanted to commence their married life together, nor the abiding memory he wished her to have—but how to avoid it?

Inspiration struck.

He tipped her chin once more, kissed the end of her nose then her lips while calculating the feasibility of his plan. Based on their previous outing to the city it seemed doable, so he asked, "But for that you would?"

Her bottom lip trembled, but her voice was steady and true. "Of course I would. I love you, Bertie."

He kissed her again. "Then we must see what we may do to circumvent your mama's plans. Perhaps we should take counsel from the Reverend Taylor on the subject? He's a good, kind man who must have come across overbearing parents before. He may have some suggestions to make."

She looked initially doubtful, but the agitation left her face, and she nodded.

He smiled. "I'll walk down to the vicarage and engage him to be at home this afternoon to see us. Meet me at the church at three?"

She returned his smile—the sweetest sight as far as he was concerned. "Yes, Bertie."

He left the kennels and did not head immediately towards the vicarage but rather to the stables, home to the horses but also the Daimler. He would certainly be calling on the Reverend Taylor, but not on foot. A visit to the Misses Hayward was also required, so he hurried through the rain, needing to get underway and onto paved roads while the dirt tracks were still firm enough to allow him to do so.

Caroline watched Bertie leave the barn. She wasn't at all sure the reverend, who was as gentle as he was kind, would be of any help, but then who knew? Bertie hadn't backed off when she'd been unable to give him an immediate yes to his proposal. He loved her and she him. It was worth a shot.

The kennel lads returned with the dogs, and as she directed them as to which obstacles to set out for the agility course, another possible solution made her spirits rise. Percy. He didn't often disoblige Mama, but if he put his foot down, she would have to desist from inviting great numbers of guests. He might not go against their mother's wishes on her behalf, he never had, but he might for Bertie, one of his closest friends.

She left the kennels shortly after one o'clock, needing to smell something other than warm, wet dog when visiting the reverend, and a violet-scented bath later, dressed in a warm flannel skirt and matching jacket, she left her room. The rain had thankfully ceased, and she found the footpath to the village to be firm enough underfoot. It occurred to her as she strode along—Bertie had said the church, but surely he'd meant the vicarage? She resolved to check the church but not to be downhearted if Bertie wasn't there. He would probably be at the vicarage where the reverend actually resided.

She needn't have worried. Bertie stood at the church door as promised. He put his arms around her when she reached him, and she tilted her face up for a kiss. His kiss was deeper than was allowable in public, but Caroline found that she didn't much care who would be scandalised if they happened to catch sight of them entwined.

They broke apart, and he smiled into her eyes. "I have a special license in my pocket, Caro. The reverend waits inside to wed us with the Misses Hayward to bear witness to our marriage vows. Just the three of them. Shall we do the deed and present the rest of the world with a fait accompli?"

Caroline's spirits took flight, her heart overflowing. *Now? This minute? With a congregation of just a couple of kind friends? Oh, yes...* She knew she must be grinning like a Cheshire cat, but then so was he. "What a wonderful idea, Bertie. It's absolutely perfect."

He offered her his arm. She threaded hers through his, and he pushed open the church door. Inside, mellow candlelight showed the Christmas roses and greenery were still in place.

Reverend Taylor stood at the head of the chancel, a welcoming smile on his face. "You tracked down the bishop and obtained the license, my lord?"

The Misses Hayward, sitting side by side in the first pew, turned around and gave a small wave.

Bertie reached into his pocket and took out a piece of folded paper. "I did. The knowledge of him liking to eat his luncheon in Tucker's Steak Shoppe you gave me this morning was invaluable, for that is exactly where I found him, thank you."

The reverend took the paper and read it. "Good. Good. All is order. Shall we begin?"

They took their places before him.

He opened his Bible and began to intone the words of the service. "Dearly Beloved, we are gathered here together…"

Bertie and Caroline repeated the required responses, and all went well until the reverend arrived at the point of blessing the ring. He paused, gazed expectantly at Bertie, and Caroline knew from the expression on Bertie's face this was a point he'd overlooked. She felt her head for a stray hairpin that could be twisted into a circle. He glanced at his own far-too-large-for-her-finger signet ring, and the Misses Hayward coughed.

"Excuse us for interrupting…"

"But when your lordship called this morning…"

"To tell us of your plans and invite us to attend the ceremony…"

"That this was one thing you didn't mention. So, we thought…"

"If you don't think it presumptuous…"

"To bring our own dear mama's gold wedding band…"

"She would be delighted to see it go forward…"

"Or used until it can be replaced with something better…"

Their kindness filled Caroline with happiness, and she left Bertie's side to plant a warm kiss on each of their cheeks. "There couldn't be anything *better*. It will be an honour to wear it if you are quite sure you can bear to part with such a precious item?"

Their faces suffused with delight, and they nodded. The reverend offered them the open Bible, and Miss Emily placed the ring upon the page. The service recommenced, and ten minutes later he pronounced them husband and wife. With a happy sigh, the new Countess of Osborne kissed her husband, then the register was duly signed by them all, and she and Bertie left the church accompanied by the earnest congratulations and good wishes of the other three.

They sauntered back to the manor, and Bertie offered, "I'll buttonhole Percy and your mother before dinner and make a clean breast of things."

Caroline stood straighter. "No, Bertie. We'll announce our marriage together standing side by side…" She looked at the man she loved, and years of pent-up longing rushed to the fore. "But not before we've spent some private time together."

He grinned. "Lady Osborne, you hussy. Lovemaking in the afternoon. How scandalous!"

She giggled. "I hope to be. You go in the front door. I'll enter by way of the kitchens. Give me half an hour to get upstairs, then come to my bedroom?"

He raised her hand to his mouth. "Willingly, my love. Drop your handkerchief on the floor outside it so I know which door to open."

Caroline dashed up the backstairs, her heart pounding. She thrust her left hand into her pocket so Jenny would not catch sight of her ring when she entered her bedroom.

Jenny was sitting by the window darning and laid her work aside. "Will you wear your cherry velvet robe or the blue this evening, my lady?"

Caroline excused her from the room. "This heavy weather has left me with a slight headache. I'll lie down on my bed for an hour or two and ring for you when I feel a little better."

Jenny bobbed her curtsey and left. She waited half a minute for her to move away then dropped a lace-edged linen square on the floor outside her room. Her heart thumped faster when she shut the door. Now that the moment had come, she realised she didn't have the first idea of how these things were supposed to go. When did one disrobe, for instance? Before the event or during it? Were the lights supposed to be on or off? Should she be reclining on the bed, or was that too forward?

She decided at last to remove her jacket and unfasten a button or two on her blouse, but as she did so it came to her that the sturdy, thick cotton, knee-length bloomers she was currently wearing due to Penelope being in the house were not the most attractive of garments. Her dressing gown, it would have to be. She stripped off and put it on, then balled up her day clothes and dumped them in the bottom of the wardrobe. There was a soft tap, and the door opened as she dabbed a drop of perfume behind each ear.

Bertie mounted the stairs to his room and could barely contain his delight. *I'm a married man!* He grinned to himself and remembered how apprehensive he'd felt about attending this house party. He had certainly not expected to fall head over heels in love, but there it was. *I have a wife!* Which was nothing short of a miracle considering the potential pitfalls of his hastily conceived plan. However, the Daimler had run perfectly, the bishop had been easily tracked down, and full of red meat and good wine, had genially agreed to Bertie's request for him to issue a special license without question or need of persuasion as to why one was necessary.

The day was still somewhat in advance of the dressing hour when he entered his room, but he decided it was close enough that if he was seen in the hallway wearing a bathrobe it would be presumed he was on his way to the bathing chamber rather than Caroline's bedroom. He left his discarded day wear on his bed knowing Ridgley, the soul of discretion he was, would tidy it away without so much as a raised eyebrow.

He left his room. His anticipation built, and he decided a quick detour to the bathroom was indeed a necessity. A large man in every respect, he could not appear in his bride's room with the stiffening erection threatening to make itself rather obvious by tenting the front of his robe. A good dousing in cold water would calm matters down for a while.

That accomplished, Bertie spotted her handkerchief and picked it up, tapped, and let himself into wife's room. His breath caught when she smiled at him. He walked to her, took her hand, and pressed his lips into her palm. She stroked her fingertips through his beard. He widened the V of his robe. Would she like the masculine downiness of the rest of him? She did.

Her fingers moved to explore the soft curls on his chest. "Oh, Bertie. How wonderful. You're all furry."

He chuckled and thought if he possessed a tail it would be wagging at double-quick speed. "As you are not?"

Caroline gazed up at him, her eyes full of trust, and opened her dressing gown. "No. I am not."

His erection refused to be denied any longer. He looked at her pert breasts and porcelain skin, her body taut from daily exercise and needing no help from any corsetry, expensive or otherwise. He lifted her into his arms and carried her to the bed, then lay beside her and kissed her long and deep. She slipped her hands inside his dressing gown and urged it off his shoulders, so he released its belt and shrugged it off.

She gazed at his manhood rising from the triangle of curls at his groin, and her eyes widened slightly. "Oooh, Bertie. Will it all fit?"

He stroked his fingers through the mound between her legs and found her wet and ready for him. "Yes, my love. I think it will." He lay over her, explored a little further, and eased his cockhead in.

She sighed when he penetrated her. "Oh, yes…"

He eased his shaft gently into the place no man had been before him.

She put her arms around his back and parted her legs. "Oh…oh…"

He kissed her lips, her neck, and flicked his tongue over her hardened nipples to her soft whimpers, so he moved his cock deeper and met the resistance of her maidenhead, then as tenderly as he could, pushed past it.

She mewled and wrapped her legs around his thighs. "Oh, Bertie. Yes…"

He increased the pace of his thrusts, and she raised her hips to meet his. The sensation built until he wasn't sure he could hold back much longer, but as soon as he thought it, Caroline arched her back and dug her fingernails into his shoulders with a low moan, leaving him free to reach his own climax.

His seed burst forth, and he groaned his pleasure. "Oh God, Caro. I love you. My beautiful wife…"

She sighed beneath him. "I love you, too."

Bertie withdrew and kissed her lips. Caroline snuggled against his side and rested her cheek on his chest. "That was wonderful. When can we do it again?"

He chuckled. "Soon. In an hour or so, if you like."

She stroked her fingers through his silky beard. "Yes, please."

Bertie kissed the top of her head and, satiated, she drowsed, secure in his embrace, relishing the muscular strength of his body against hers, until with a tap on the door, Percy's voice sounded from the other side of it.

"Caro. Caro. Did Bertie tell you anything of his plans for today? He disappeared in the Daimler this morning and hasn't been seen since. He surely can't desert a house party on New Year's Eve?"

She looked up, and Bertie mouthed, "Damn. The Daimler's still at the vicarage."

She suppressed a giggle, then to her horror, the door handle began to turn. "Caro. Are you in here…?"

Percy never came into her room. What a time for him to change his mind. Bertie urged her head beneath the covers, and nothing loath, she ducked out of sight and left the men to sort the matter out. She nearly giggled again, though, when she heard the surprise in her brother's voice.

"Bertie? Is that you? What are you doing in Caro's bed? You and she haven't…? Oh Lord, you have, haven't you? Sorry, old boy, but you'll have to marry her now."

Her husband's reply delighted her. "We're already married, Piggy. By special license, this afternoon. So, if you wouldn't mind departing my wife's bedroom, we'll be with you shortly, I'm sure."

Percy let out a triumphant whoop. "There are a couple of bottles of vintage champers laid down for just such an occasion. I'll get Johnstone to break 'em out of the wine cellar."

Caroline let go of her giggles as soon as the door closed, then surfaced for air. "The whole house will be privy to our news in about ten minutes from now."

Bertie smiled. "Good. It saves us the trouble of announcing it. We should still go down and make our peace with your mother, though. If you're sure you can face it?"

She nodded. "With you at my side, yes. Just don't let Penelope sneak up behind me?"

He frowned. "Why? What does she do?"

"She's older than me, bigger than me, and always was. It amuses her to make be blush. If she can get away with it unnoticed, she'll shove me in the small of my back, hoping I'll trip and my skirts will flip up, exposing my unmentionables for the delectation of all those present."

Bertie's face looked thunderous, and he growled. "No wonder you don't care for overcrowded rooms where you can't see her coming."

She snuggled closer and admitted, "Crinolines were the worst. Those wretched hoops I wore beneath them would tip at the least provocation."

He tightened his arms around her. "I won't leave your side, and she won't get past me."

Caroline smiled at her man-mountain. "I know it."

Bertie kissed her. "I'd best go and tog up. Will an hour be sufficient for you to do the same?"

She nodded. He swung his legs off the bed and donned his bathrobe. She watched him leave the room before doing the same. As she suspected, the bedsheet with its tell-tale stain needed disposing of, and not by way of the gossiping laundry maids. She pulled it from the bed, folded it, and rang the bell for Jenny.

Her maid arrived in less than ten minutes. "Are you recovered from your headache, my lady?"

Caroline couldn't keep the wide smile from her face. "I am and must apologise for my subterfuge. Lord Osborne and I recently discovered a mutual attraction. The Reverend Taylor wed us earlier this afternoon."

Jenny's eyes widened. Her mouth became a round 'O'. Her eyes flicked towards the sheet, then to the gold band adorning Caroline's left hand. "Love-a-duck, my lady. You never did?"

Caroline's happiness bubbled up, and she laughed. "I did. I really did. I am now the Countess of Osborne and married to the most wonderful man."

Jenny, having already stepped outside the boundary of mistress and maid, grinned. "Well, strike me stupid for not noticing what was going on. Give me that linen. It'll be on the furnace shortly, and I'll remake your bed. When are we leaving Avondale Manor? I know I could do with a change of scene."

Caroline handed over her bundle and squeezed Jenny's hand. "You wish to depart with me then?"

Jenny smiled. "I would like nothing better, my lady. Are you taking your supper in the library? Shall I lay out your cherry velvet or the blue?"

Caroline squared her shoulders and prepared to meet her new responsibilities head-on. "No. My husband and I will attend Mama in the drawing room this evening. I'll wear my grey watered silk."

The most glamorous outfit she possessed was more a silver-grey than the dull rain-cloud shade of the colour and was comprised of a tightly fitting bolero jacket worn over a camisole of white lace with a matching skirt. Jenny re-dressed her hair which during the afternoon had come to resemble a bird's nest, then departed with the bedsheet tucked under her arm.

Bertie tapped on the door not long after and smiled when he saw her. "You look beautiful, my love. Shall we go down?"

Caroline swallowed hard and linked her arm through his. "Yes, we should. I'm ready."

They walked down the stairs, and her nerves jangled, but with Bertie at her side she felt more assured. He reached into his pocket and pulled out a silver half-crown when they reached the hall. Alfie, the footman on the chair, jumped to attention.

Bertie handed him the coin. "Announce us, if you please? The Marquis of Osborne and his wife, the Countess of Osborne."

Alfie grinned. "As loud as you like, your lordship."

Bertie patted his shoulder. "Good man. Go to it."

They followed Alfie, and he threw open the double doors of the drawing room with great aplomb. Heads turned as he made his announcement, and she froze. Bertie squeezed her hand and coaxed her forward. Mama's was the first face she saw.

She dabbed her eyes and gushed, "Oh, my dears. I'm so happy. So naughty of you not to tell me. What a wonderful New Year's surprise."

Behind her, Percy winked and toasted them with his champagne glass. Mr and Mrs Budleigh-Benson appeared delighted, probably because their hostess was, but Penelope stood beside them, and her face had a noticeable absence of a smile.

Their nuptials given the seal of approval by her mother and brother, other guests crowded around and offered their congratulations. Immovable as a rock, Bertie rested his hand protectively on the small of her back, but unnoticed in midst of the throng, Penelope sidled up to her other side and hissed, "Do you really imagine you'll be enough to satisfy a man like that, little mouse? I give you three months. Then he'll be back in Town touring the salons, searching for a proper woman to meet his needs."

Bertie, as promised, must have been keeping a wary eye out, though. He slipped his arm around her waist, urged her closer to his side, and glowered at Penelope. "I am not naturally a vindictive man, but if you ever approach my wife in that manner again, I will put the word around the gentleman's clubs in Town of your being an indiscreet, presumptuous blabbermouth. Thereafter, I promise, you will find yourself regrettably short of invitations to attend anything, anywhere in the future."

Penelope looked furious at being caught out. Her mouth opened, but before she could utter another word, Bertie, his face a picture of utter disdain, turned away.

"Come, my love. Let's eat our supper together elsewhere."

Caroline was nothing but happy to comply, and with her head held high, accompanied him out of the room. She guessed their destination—the library—but was surprised to see a bottle of champagne cooling in an ice bucket along with a luxurious buffet selection that included thinly sliced smoked salmon and caviar.

Bertie smiled. "Cheeky of me, I know. But I dispatched my man, Ridgley, to make Johnstone and Cook privy to our news. They were more than pleased to arrange this for us."

Caroline giggled. "Bertie!"

He appeared not one wit abashed, poured the champagne, and chinked his glass on hers. "We stand on the brink of a new decade, so cheers and bottoms up to nineteen-hundred and ten and the start of our life together."

Caroline toasted him back, mentally consigning the previous decade onto the rubbish heap of dreadfulness. The nineteen-tens. How modern that sounded. A whole new era of happiness stretched out before her. No storm clouds loomed on the horizon to spoil the vista. She and Bertie were in love, and nothing, but nothing could spoil the wonderful life they would have together.

Could it…?

The Darling Dowager's Christmas Treat

Raven McAllan

Chapter One

Nicholas Stanstead, the Earl of Littlethorpe, stood hidden behind a curtain, in the shadows of the antechamber, unseen by the other two occupants.

He however could see them clearly, as the candlelight illuminated their faces.

One, his elder brother, had accosted the elegantly dressed lady who now stood, arms akimbo, and berated the man.

"You," she said scornfully, "would not know a reasoned and responsible reply if it hit you in the face. Listen well to me. No, no, and never."

Good for you, my lady. And to say all those words beginning with 'r' and 'n' and not stutter is truly amazing. He listened on, not at all ashamed at eavesdropping. Sometimes, he thought, needs must. Why on earth had she let herself be inveigled in that way?

The duke, his elder brother, smiled patronisingly. "You have been out of mourning long enough. It is time for you to remarry, and I will be the perfect husband for you. I'll do all that is necessary." He took her hand and lifted it to his lips before he gripped her shoulders. "I will put the notice in *The Times* tomorrow."

"You," the lady pointed at him with the hand he hadn't touched, "are addled. Too much brandy."

Very likely, and inferior gut-rot I would wager.

"Watch my lips carefully," the lady continued in clipped tones. "And listen well."

Oh, I will, and very kissable they are, too.

She tugged her hand out of the duke's, took a step backwards, and glanced at her now freed hand as if it might be contaminated. Then she

84

stared directly at him, her palms planted firmly on her hips. One shoe-clad foot tapped out a staccato, impatient rhythm on the parquetry floor.

"You will do no such thing. Not tomorrow, not ever. No...do you understand?" she demanded in a voice designed to cut a person to ribbons.

As the unseen witness, Nicholas winced on behalf of his brother, the recipient, even though it sounded as if he didn't deserve it.

"No, I will *not marry you,*" she went on in that same clipped tone. "No, I do *not* want to marry again, and if, *if* I ever did, it would not be to a pompous, stuffed-up, full-of-his-own-importance windbag such as you. *Do* you understand? I believe I speak in clear, basic English. You ride roughshod over everyone, ignore everything except what you want. Always you, you, and you. Let me say this, you may be an aristocrat, but believe me, you are no gentleman."

The duke's face went red. "How dare you."

Nicholas watched his brother's hand tighten on the lady's shoulder and tensed, ready to intervene if necessary.

There was no need.

"Oh, I dare, Your Grace. Now take you hands off me before I scream."

Don't do that, I'd have to come out of the shadows and do something, which would probably be very embarrassing to both of you.

The duke dropped his hands. "You are overwrought. Should I send for your carriage?"

"Not unless it is to run you down!" she snapped then sighed. "Your Grace, I have tried to put you off politely. It didn't work, so I have to be more forceful. But please, listen carefully. I will not be your duchess. Not now, not ever. And if you try to force my hand, you will soon discover it will be to your detriment. Now, I suggest you go back to the ballroom before someone comes in and you try to turn that to your advantage. I am no green miss, and I can *not* be forced into anything I do not wish to do. Marriage is one of them."

The duke smiled patronisingly and patted her shoulder before he took a hasty step back. "I can see it will take you a while to understand your good fortune. I'll call on you tomorrow to discuss how we proceed. I suggest we marry in the New Year, here in town, where there will be no problem to get to the church. That gives you a few weeks to organise what you need to do. Of course, my estate would be preferable, but one must make sacrifices."

The lady's eyes widened. "You…you…insufferable egoist, one most certainly will not. Because if you try to do any of that, you will wish you hadn't. I will make certain that not only are you refused admittance, I will make you even more of a laughing-stock than you already are." She took a deep breath, and her rather magnificent bosom swelled under the low neckline of her ballgown. "Now, try to be enough of a man to go away. Now. At once. Before I hit you."

You tell him, my dear. And please, breathe deeper, go on.

Sadly, she didn't. *Damn.*

"My dear…" Was that a hint of a whine? Probably—as things didn't seem to be running smoothly for his brother.

Has he he always sounded so pompous? Nicholas thought about it for a second. Indeed he had. *My pompous, self-centred, short-sighted brother, who thinks the world owes him a living, and never considers the opinion of anyone else is of any importance.*

"I am *not* and never will be your dear, or, in fact, your anything unless you consider nemesis," the lady said with contempt. "Get out of my sight." She crossed her arms and tapped her foot once more.

Nicholas loved her attitude. He wished he could show her just how much.

His wish was granted.

The duke bowed stiffly. "Until tomorrow at noon, my dear." He left the room as the lady gave a muted scream.

"Argh, of all the…" She stopped tapping and stamped her foot instead, as if she wished it were the duke she was stamping on.

Nicholas rather thought that was in her mind.

He waited until the door closed at the back of his brother and emerged from behind the curtain, clapping as he did so.

The lady whirled round with a flurry of silken skirts.

"You? That's all I need. Why are you here?" She pointed her finger at him, accusingly. "If you are found there could be mayhem."

He understood that, but information had showed him he had to be ready for intervention if it was needed.

"Now is that any way to speak to your saviour?" he drawled. "Not very grateful, my dear."

She rolled her eyes, something Nicholas was envious of.

"What did you save me from?" she enquired. "I saw nothing that would require your intervention."

"It was the fact I could have if I had to that matters."

"If you say so. Thank you." She looked towards the curtains. "Do you perhaps need to leave the way I assume you came in? It's rather draughty in here, so no doubt the window is still open. It best be closed before I catch my death or someone else appears."

"Of course, and along with your thanks, I'll take my reward." Nicholas pinned her arms to her sides, bent his head, and kissed her deeply.

Her scent surrounded him, enveloping him in what he always thought as the essence of her. His cock rose to the occasion, stretched his pantaloons to the limit, and was in danger of a severe chafing, when it was only quick thinking that saved him from having her knee in his genitals and her teeth through his tongue.

Nicholas drew back. "Nasty. Termagant," he said in a voice laced with humour. "Never lose that edge."

"I thought *he* was bad, but at least he didn't force himself on me," she said scornfully.

Nicholas let go of her wrists.

"Nor did I," he drawled. "You responded for at least five seconds before you decided you shouldn't. Think about that."

He bowed and moved back towards the curtained window alcove, where he had stood before. "I am always around for you if need be."

She gave a sad smile as he turned away. Her words, whispered so quietly, only just reached him.

"Ah, if only that were the way of it."

Chapter Two

Sometimes, Isabella thought, she must be saddle pated. Who on earth, in their right mind, would set off from London, a mere sennight or so before Christmas, to head to the wilds of Yorkshire, with a sky full of snow and only her trusted coachmen as companions?

Evidently, she, Isabella Maria, The Dowager Duchess of Lewes, would.

There were, of course, mitigating circumstances, in the form of one Gregory Stanstead, Duke of Ancaster, who would not understand or accept she had no thoughts of remarriage, and if she ever did, it would not be to him.

Ancaster was the sort of man she abhorred. The type of man, Stephen, her late husband, called a bag of bloated, humourless, human nature. Rude, but oh how it fitted. Pompous, puffed up, and full of self-importance. The sort of man who once he had made his mind up about something, he assumed it would automatically happen.

The sort of man who, when anything around him was not to his liking, he ignored it. Metaphorically stamped his foot, pouted, and sulked, to then assume once more his word would be law.

The sort of man who, due to his lack of comprehension and his inability to understand the word no, had forced her to undertake the journey. Which meant she would not be where she wanted to be to enjoy Christmas for the first time since she came out of mourning and decided it was time to take the reins of her life once more.

He was not the sort of man to cause her heart to quicken, and her pulse race, or her body tingle, and half-forgotten sensations emerge. Or the sort of man she could ever contemplate spending even one day of her life with, let alone the rest of it, however long that might be.

That was reserved for the one man she knew she could never have. Who she dare not involve in her problems.

To whit, not the man who had intimated he would call on her again, that day, and thus was the reason for her unwanted trip north, to the cottage her godmother left her in a village near Ripon. Isabella had managed to visit a few times each year since her marriage and subsequent widowhood, and knew it would be ready for her when she arrived. Even if it weren't, she would cope somehow. Bowmans was her bolthole, and she was fairly sure it was not generally known outwith its immediate area, that she was the owner.

Jeanne—the friend who aided Isabella's escape from the capital—had included some root vegetables in the portmanteau she had provided, as well as a few ounces of precious tea and some flour. It might be plain fare, but she wouldn't starve. Luckily, years ago Isabella's godmama had shown Isabella some plain cookery recipes, all of which had been useful when she had, to the scandalous astonishment of many, accompanied her Army General husband to the continent in the early days of the Napoleonic wars.

It had been dirty, hard-going, rough-and-ready conditions, and she had loved every moment of them until Stephen, worried at how desperate things had become, sent her home, just before Waterloo, where sadly he lost his life.

Strange how she had coped with those days both before and after Stephen's death but couldn't find a way out of her present predicament except to flee.

Her late husband's voice echoed around her mind. *"Sometimes it is better to retreat and regroup, wiser and more prepared."*

Perceptive words, and ones she intended to follow to the letter.

Isabella mulled over what she had achieved so far. She hadn't dare send notice of her intentions to Bowman Manor—somewhat of a misnomer, cottage was more like it—her destination—just in case someone else got hold of them. It was a pity, but she couldn't be certain someone in her household wasn't sharing details of her whereabouts. If that were the case, and for example the damned duke got hold of them, he would have once more done as he wanted and ignored everything else.

Hopefully once there, she could gather greenery and make the place as cheerful as possible for Christmas. Plus, if her loyal coachmen and Vickers, her major domo, thought it safe, those of her staff who had no family elsewhere, or chose not to stay in London, would, with luck, arrive the day before Christmas. The timing was tight but possible.

As long as the dratted snow stopped and the false information she had asked Vicars to impart to her maid, who she had a feeling would share it, and a few others who he knew would *not* pass it on except at his direction, worked.

The thought of that pest Ancaster following her and pressing his suit once more made her go hot and cold. She'd had enough of him for a lifetime.

His brother, however…

Isabella pondered over what the ton called the mysterious case of the duke's younger brother, the Earl of Littlethorpe. Where he was, or what he was up to, nobody appeared to know.

If Ancaster did, he either didn't care or wasn't prepared to share the information.

Out of sight, out of mind? Knowing Ancaster, that was the most likely scenario. Stephen had always insisted there was more to the estrangement than met the eye. However, he had kept his council and never shared his thoughts on the matter with Isabella, except to say Nicholas was a good man to have in your corner. And, he had added with a wink, a ladies' man par excellence.

Isabella had very little idea about that, except... She put her hand to her lips as she remembered that hot-and-heady kiss.

Outrageous. How dare he?

Nevertheless, oh, how glad she was he *had* dared. If nothing else, it reminded her she was a warm-blooded woman, who did have feelings and was no ice maiden as some repulsed gentlemen had intimated.

As the first snowflakes descended, her coach reached the inn where it had been decided they should change horses. She left the relative warmth of the coach for a cup of hot chocolate and the facilities, and decided she couldn't blame Nicholas Stanstead for removing himself from his brother's orbit. Any sane person would.

As she hoped she had done.

The duke was an idiot. There could be no other reason for such an arrogant and unyielding attitude.

The farther she got from London, the happier she became. Isabella left the inn and headed for her carriage again, where, it seemed, it had been no time at all before new horses were harnessed and were now ready and waiting. She climbed in and was on the move once more a minute later.

With a last glance at the snow, still settling but not too heavily, thank goodness, Isabella pulled her cloak around her more tightly and rested her feet on the flannel-wrapped hot brick the thoughtful landlord had provided. That, along with a fur-lined rug, meant she was snug inside, although she pitied her poor coachmen out in the open. They, who had served at Waterloo with her late husband, were loyal and trustworthy. It was Clumber, her head coachman, who had told her not to mention where they were headed, and had even driven out of town by a circuitous route. Just in case, he intimated that somehow, whereabouts were shared. Hence her false trail.

It was an uncomfortable feeling, wondering if someone in your household was not to be depended on to keep confidences. Nevertheless,

Isabella could see no other reason why the duke dogged her footsteps and appeared to know where she would be and when. Therefore, as far as the rest of her household was concerned, she had, at that moment, merely gone to her dressmakers to have a new gown made and a favourite one altered. When her maid, Bessie, newly appointed and always overeager to please had said, worriedly, she'd need a companion, and it wouldn't be seemly for her to go alone especially as…and then stopped speaking in a rush, Isabella's suspicions had been roused. For once, she was short with the girl and said she would do as she pleased.

"If a dowager can't go to her dressmaker without gossip and scandal, I wonder what the world is coming to. I will return via Hatchards."

She made a beeline for Bruton Street, entered the establishment of Madame Jeanne—modiste—and half an hour later, exited via the back door, across the yard, and into the mews where the carriage waited for her.

Madame Jeanne, born Jeanie Plaskett on Isabella's papa's estate, was waiting for her with a valise containing small clothes and enough gowns and cloaks for Isabella to be comfortable for a few weeks at least.

"And there's toothpowder, a brush and comb, and some hairpins," Madame Jeanne said. "Plus a nightrail, a pair of half boots that should fit, and a book or two like you said when we last met. Mind you, I never expected to get the letter, which gave me notice of your intentions. To say if you said you wanted a puce gown, it was our code for leaving now, was inspired. No one but us would know just how much you dislike the colour."

The duke was partial to puce-striped waistcoats.

Isabella got a Gothic novel out of her bag, wriggled to make herself comfortable in the corner of her coach, and began to read, thus to pass the time until their overnight stop.

It was, she thought, as the short winter's day began to draw to a close, lucky she was no longer considered a young lady who needed a companion or chaperone. Now at nine and twenty, she was an old maid, an ape leader, and a dowager to boot. How her beloved Stephen would laugh at that description.

How she missed him, although she was conscious that even before he was killed, they were changing in oh so different ways. She, at ten years his junior, was years ahead of him in maturity. Would that difference have increased and caused friction? She would never know. With a sigh deep enough to rattle the fabric of the coach, Isabella glanced out of the window and wondered exactly where they were.

Her coachmen had advised her not to travel by the Great North Road. That was the way most people would head north, plus it was also on the way to Ancaster's ancestral home. Instead, they and she had decided on less-travelled roads. It meant there was a better chance that if need be, she could pass as a lady's companion on her way to a new appointment. Not seen and recognised as the Dowager Duchess of Lewes but accepted without comment as Miss Bella Ripley, governess or whatever. If it meant an extra day on her journey to ensure she got to her destination without being accosted, so be it. She would rather be safe than sorry.

Their circuitous way was the reason that by the time they arrived at Long's Inn, it was nigh on dark, the snow was falling faster and lay a good two inches on the ground. Isabella was bone weary, chilled, and felt grubby. Thank goodness she had taken the chance to book accommodation in advance.

The inn, although not on a major coaching road, nor frequented by the aristocracy, was snug, well-appointed, and with a reputation for being safe. It was also well-known for its excellent food and overnight facilities for both humans and horses. Isabella was glad to alight and let her coachmen talk to the ostler and arrange for the animals to be stabled.

The room she was allocated was not the level she would have expected as a duchess in a more exclusive inn, but much more superior to that to which most companions would be allotted. She could not fault it. Clean, tidy, and a bright fire burned in the grate, which warmed the room. It was no bother to take off her cloak and wash in the hot water provided. Once she was dressed once more, now in a simple, cosy woollen gown—thanks to Madame Jeanne—she was ready to wait for her dinner.

Which she was to eat in her room.

"For we're a bit busy, ma'am, due to the weather, and mebbes you'd be happier there?"

the landlord had said in a hopeful voice. "Might get a bit rowdy in the dining room, and our one private room is out of action. Been a bit of a flood there. Best snug upstairs."

"Oh, yes, what a good idea," Isabella had said gratefully. She had no wish to be seen by anyone who might recognise her and remember if they were subsequently questioned. "That would suit me perfectly."

They had agreed on a mutton broth, followed by roast chicken and root vegetables, and as the landlord put it, a nice filling apple pie to finish, along with some cheese from the farm down the lane, all accompanied by his wife's homemade cowslip wine. It, Isabella discovered, packed a rather welcoming punch.

She got into bed, somewhat mellow, replete, and ready to sleep. Which she did until the chambermaid brought her morning coffee and washing water.

"Busy downstairs, it is," the girl said chattily. "The snow ain't so bad, it stopped around midnight so the landlord says. You'll be fine on the roads as long as you avoid those tiddly ones. The one down to me ma's is fair awful. Almost out of milk now, we are, so hope me pa can get up with the cart later or we'll be a bit pushed." She laughed. "At least we've plenty of ale. Where you off to, if I may be so bold as to ask?"

Isabella thought rapidly. "Chelmsford," she said, naming the first town she could think of in the wrong direction. "My papa is gravely ill. His employer sent for me, it is feared he will not last above a few days."

"There now," the maid said in a sympathetic voice. "Let's pray to our Lord you get there in time. I'll bring your breakfast in a few minutes, shall I, and you can be on your way in under the hour. Should I tell the coachmen?"

Isabella nodded. "If you please."

Chapter Three

"So you see, m'lord, I thought it best to tell you now, so we can plan."

Nicholas looked up from paring his nails and raised both eyebrows. To his chagrin, he could never manage to raise just one in the manner a certain lady of his acquaintance could.

"We?" he queried.

Bascombe, Nicholas's manservant and right-hand man, nodded. "Certainly we, my lord, if you would be so good as to allow it. Standing, the head groom, Michael, the under groom, Billings," the gardener, who could turn his hand to anything, "and myself."

"Am I allowed to ask how you found this out?" Nicholas replied to Bascombe as the man folded cravats and put them neatly in a drawer. "Who has a foot in both camps, so to speak?"

"No one, my lord. Unless you count the fact that my second cousin, Freddie, is employed by the duke in a very menial capacity and keeps his ears open. There are rumours abound in the household that His Grace expects to bring home a wife very soon. Ah…" He coughed delicately. "It seems whilst in his cups he was heard to say if she wasn't prepared to accept he was the man for her, he would just have to persuade her. Then he muttered something about the Abbey and preparation."

Carnbelton Abbey was their ancestral home, now of course the home of Gregory, and no longer Nicholas.

Nicholas tapped his teeth with his paring knife, saw Bascombe's disapproving expression, and stopped. "Yes, a disgusting habit, I agree, you are right to glare at me like that. I must endeavour not to do it."

"I never glare," Bascombe said in a composed manner. "But I agree with you that you should desist. A lady would not find it agreeable."

Nicholas nodded; it was a reasonable comment. Or that the only lady he would even consider in his bedchamber was ever likely to see it, or his paring knife. "So, we have a spy in my brother's household? Does he have one here?"

"He most certainly does not," Bascombe said, unperturbed. "As for in his establishment? Not so much a spy, my lord, but someone who is earnest in their support of justice. After all the rumours that are flying around, with regards to your brother's marriage, and what you mentioned to me recently, I thought it sensible to ask Freddie to, ahem, let me know what was going on." He coughed. "He didn't want to be disloyal to his employer, but as he has already been treated abysmally by His Grace... A matter of time off rescinded at short notice and a general lack of good manners towards his staff, I believe. His Grace is not the most popular of employers, and I think Freddie will be looking for new employment before long." He carefully shut the drawer where he had placed the cravats and began to tidy the top of the chest of drawers.

"He," Bascombe said with diffidence, "I believe is a wonder with horses."

Nicholas nodded. "We'll see what we can do when this is over. Did he say anything else?"

"That His Grace ordered his carriage for tomorrow and to be prepared to head to the Abbey until he returned with his wife. He had enough shilly-shallying from her. That I believe was to himself, but he has a habit of speaking out loud quite forcefully, and anyone in the vicinity can't but help hear. Freddie was carrying a jug of ale to him when that information was inadvertently disclosed."

"I thank you." Nicholas thought for a moment. "Ah, do we know where the lady in question is?"

"We know she is not where she purports to be," Bascombe said. "The duke was in a veritable temper when he discovered that."

"I bet he was," Nicholas said with relish. "Do we have any ideas?"

"It seems she went to the modiste's and ah, slipped out of the back door. Madame Jeanne was wide-eyed and innocent, and His Grace incandescent with rage. He has people checking every way out of the capital." Bascombe shook his head. "It doesn't look good."

It didn't. Nicholas stood, tied his cravat, and let Bascombe help him into his waistcoat and jacket. He had an ace up his sleeve. "I will pay a visit to Madame Jeanne. Arrange for..." He paused. By himself he would have used his curricle for speed, but should he take a carriage? No, speed was needed. "...my curricle to be made ready and prepare to follow me with the lightweight carriage, to Russets unless I send word different." Russets was his country home in the North Riding of Yorkshire. Almost as far from his ancestral acres as could be. "I'll hail a handsome cab to the modiste's."

What a way to spend the week before Christmas.

Nicholas thought of the date with a jolt. "You better tell the staff I may not be around for Christmas, and their boxes will be given to them by Black." His major domo. Nicholas thought over his options. "Once I've spoken to Madame Jeanne, I'll know better what I'm going to do. I should be back within a couple of hours. Can you make sure I've got enough clothes packed for a sennight at least?"

"Of course, my lord. Where are we going?"

109

"We're not, I may be." Nicholas picked up his hat. "Don't look like that. If I need you I will send for you. I promise." He nodded and headed out.

"And what, my lord, do you expect from me?" Madame Jeanne crossed her arms and inclined her head to the interested maid who hovered in the doorway. "That will be all, Annie, thank you."

Madame Jeanne narrowed her eyes in warning to Nicholas and waited until the maid, with a distinct toss of the head and a flounce, left the room.

Nicholas opened his mouth to speak, and Madame Jeanne put her finger over her lips. He nodded, interested to see what she intended to do.

She waited three seconds, slipped off her shoes, and walked to the door and flung it open. To catch Annie as she almost fell into the room.

"As I thought, Annie Button." Madame Jeanne pointed at the maid who sniffed, sobbed, and looked sideways to see how her attitude affected both Nicholas and her employer.

Madame Jeanne was unaffected, and Nicholas smiled.

"Doesn't work, Miss Annie," he said. "Crocodile tears."

"That was your last chance, Annie Button." Madame Jeanne shook her head. "Loyalty and tight lips are what is needed in a modiste's establishment. *Which* you have been reminded about on numerous occasions. Not someone who thinks to eavesdrop and earn a penny with their tittle-tattle. Fine way to repay me. Mrs Madden will give you your wages. Enough, you no longer work here."

"He said as if I sort of found out what the lady was up to he'd be good to me." Annie rubbed her nose on the back of her hand. "What'll I do now?"

Nicholas shuddered and sighed with relief as Madame Jeanne handed the girl a strip of rag.

"Wipe your nose. You should have thought of that before you chose to betray me." The words were laced with scorn and, Nicholas deduced, hurt.

Annie snuffled and blew her nose with a trumpet.

Nicholas's ears rang at the noise. It jarred.

"You don't let me do much, so I thought why not," Annie whined. "I'm sick of being the one without anything."

"You don't do much because you aren't capable," Jeanne retorted. "Nor do you wish to learn. Now go, and let's hope he is as good as his word."

"He's a duke, he will be." She threw the rag on the floor. "And I'll make sure his wife won't come here never ever."

"It is not likely that he will be good or even remember what she lost because of him," Nicholas said as the weeping woman left. "But not our problem. I could apologise on behalf of my brother but I'm damned if I see why I should."

Jeanne nodded. "Nor should you. He and that cursed Annie are at fault, not you, and sadly, she pays the price for her greed. I reward loyalty not betrayal. I won't see her destitute but nor will I reward her, *or* forget her perfidy. She can go home to her parents or do as she wishes. So, my lord, what do you want?"

Nicholas blinked at the abrupt change of topic and grinned. "Come on, Jeannie, enough of the 'my lord'. A friend of yours is in a fix with my arrogant, antagonistic brother, which is no doubt why Annie was bribed to discover what she could. We need to help the lady."

"Really?" she said with a quizzical expression. "We?"

"We," he confirmed. "As in, you and me."

"What's in it for you?" she asked. "It might help me make up my mind."

Time to confess. "I have loved the lady since I first saw her," Nicholas said with frank honesty. "I was at school with her husband's younger brother, I served with her husband." His expression was bleak. "I was wounded and watched him die. I crawled, Jeannie, I bloody crawled over dead and dying men, but I got to him too late. I could do naught to save him. How could she ever forgive me for that? If all I can do is look out for her and save her from my brother's clutches, then I will."

Jeannie nodded, and it seemed, made her mind up. "Good idea. She is headed for her house in Yorkshire."

"Yorkshire? She has a house there?" He hadn't known that. "Fortuitous," he murmured.

Madame Jeanne inclined her head. "Indeed. I'll get you the address. She decided not to go straight up the Great North Road so will take a day longer to get there." She rummaged in a drawer for some paper and a pencil. "I have heard rumours that your brother is somewhat short of the readies," she said delicately. "Do you know anything about that?"

"Damn." Nicholas slammed his fist down on the cupboard so the contents inside rattled and the vase and bowl on top jumped. "Of course, that must be it. Jeannie, you remember when I was, to put no finer point on it, ostracised and in effect expelled from my family and wouldn't say why?"

She nodded. "You were in despair and well on your way to being a sot."

Nicholas inclined his head in agreement. It had been a hard and harrowing time. Jeannie had been a godsend. "Until you sorted me out. I never disclosed why I behaved as I did. It was too close to my heart and showed a member of my family in a very dishonourable light, but you deserve the truth. It was because Gregory thought I should hand my inheritance and monies over to him. I refused. Since then, I have never visited my home, and we have never spoken. In fact, his animosity was so bad, I've kept well out of his orbit. Especially since I was informed by, shall we say, someone less than reputable to the polite word but a true friend to me, that he had put a price on my head. He, of course, is my next of kin." He smiled. "I put it about I'd spent all my money, I was destitute, and the only thing anyone, including my heir, would receive from my demise was to inherit my debts and win a trip to the gallows."

He paused and grinned. "I think it worked."

Chapter Four

Another evening and another inn was in her immediate future. Isabella was heartily sick of travelling. She felt grimy and uncomfortable and was certain the seat in the coach, that when she had left London, was the epitome of comfort had somehow been switched to one full of nails.

Her bottom had suffered. Even when she folded one of the rugs up and sat on it as well, her rear ached.

Thank goodness her coachmen had intimated they should reach their destination the following day. "Well before sunset, and in time to do what's needed, my lady. We could push on, but is it really worth it?"

Isabella had agreed it was not and resigned herself to another night in an inn. However, never before had Isabella heard such welcome words as 'almost there'. The day had seemed endless, with most of it spent in the coach. Their last change of horses had been a lengthy one, due to one losing a shoe just after it had been poled up. That meant they had to wait for a substitute. She had been told it was only two hours or so before they would reach The Red Lion where a welcome bed and a hot meal awaited. Isabella had never been so happy about anything. The snow had eased somewhat, but the biting, icy wind had not. She was cold, tired, and ready for a hot bath, a hot meal, and a warm bed. In that order.

Isabella closed the book she had been trying to read—with little success. The heroine was insipid, the hero hectoring, and he reminded her of the duke. Not someone she wished to read about—especially in the guise of a so-called hero. More likely an archenemy in her mind.

The road was snow-packed, with icy patches and more uneven than the coachmen said it would normally be. She had to reiterate and reassure them that she thought they still had done the correct thing by travelling on it and not the Great North Road. However, an incipient headache was making its presence known, no doubt due to her having been jolted for several hours. She tossed her hat onto the seat, wriggled until she was tight up against the corner of the carriage, and shut her eyes. Perhaps a snooze would help.

It may well have done.

Isabella had no idea how long it was until she was woken with a start as the carriage lurched right, jumped—as did her heart—then tilted to the left and came to a halt at a rather uncomfortable angle. She slid to one end of the bench seat—sadly, the end where it was hardest to get out of the carriage—and swore. What in Hades had happened?

"My lady, are you all right?" The face of her head coachman appeared in the window aperture as his shoulders and the rest of his body blocked the lowering sun. "Bloody kids, I reckon.

Laid wood over the road, little varmints. Joe's getting rid of it. We'll soon get you sorted."

Isabella ground her teeth and bit back the epithet she really wanted to utter. 'I'm fine, what…?" She lost her train of thought, as there was a shout outside somewhere and her coachman disappeared. "What is it?"

The outline of a different head filled the window space and darkened her vision once more. "Not what, who. Me. Out you get."

That sounded like… "Nicholas? What the *hell* are you playing at?"

"Not playing, my dear," he said in a voice that intimated unfailing intent. "This is deadly earnest. I think it needs to be me here to talk to you now, or it will be my brother later who disturbs you. Your choice."

Isabella assimilated his words. *What?* "I've had a bang on the head," she said. "I must be hallucinating, there can be no other reason why I think I can see and hear the Earl of Littlethorpe, here, talking to me in the middle of a tiny road well away from everywhere. He's never around, makes a point of it, so it must be my imagination. Or, wait, perhaps it is a nightmare?"

The nightmare laughed. "Call me what you wish, my love, but listen well. My brother intends to waylay you in the morning and take you to the Abbey. Whether he thinks to ruin you and wed you, or uphold your honour and wed you, I have no idea. I have, however, been given to understand that he intends to return home with a wife. To whit, you."

Isabella blinked and pushed her hair out of her eyes. It was sounding more farcical by the moment.

Or did it? If she truly thought that, why was she fleeing?

First things first. She thought quickly.

"Is my carriage drivable?" she asked prosaically. That seemed to be the most pressing problem. The duke, his intentions, her reactions, and following actions could wait. "Can we move?"

"It will be fine once we right it. I made sure there was no chance of it tipping over any more than it has already," Nicholas said. "If you give me leave, we will help your coachmen right it."

"We?" Isabella queried. "Who is 'we'?"

"Myself and some of my loyal staff, one of whom first told me of my brother's intentions. He has a relative who overheard my brother in his cups. He—my brother, not the relative—has a habit of talking to himself. The more he imbibes, the louder he gets. It was thought, thankfully, that the information needed to be shared with me. Hence, here I am. So? Your decision?"

"Right the carriage," Isabella said. "Please. Then we can talk." And she could get to her next accommodation, have a bath, and relax for a short while.

And think what next?

The *bloody* duke. Why could he not be gentleman enough to take no for an answer?

"Hold on tight, it will not take long."

Nicholas was as good as his word. He disappeared from view, and her world—and the carriage—rocked, and then she and it were upright again. The door opened, and Nicholas stood in the opening.

"May I come in so we can talk?" he enquired. "It's bloody cold out here, and I fear we are due for more snow. A white Christmas appears to be in the offing."

"Then shouldn't we head for the inn?" Isabella asked. "I would hate to be stuck on the road."

"If once you have heard me out, then I will give instructions for you to be taken there. However…" Nicholas paused and sighed. "Do you trust me?"

"Of course I do," Isabella said without a second thought, then started. "I do, but I do not know why, except Stephen said he would trust you with his life. Therefore, it seems sensible to trust you with mine. Even though there is something mysterious going on between you and your damned brother."

"Damned is exactly what he is," Nicholas said soberly. "He needs money and fast. Hence his desire to marry you. A rich widow, in his words not mine, something I will emphasise, who I understand he has said is 'ripe for the plucking'."

"Repellent person. He thinks he would marry me and have my money to waste?" Isabella laughed. "If only he knew. As it should be, most of the estate was entailed and is now in the able hands of Stephen's cousin, Geoffrey. My money is only mine until I remarry. Then it is held in trust until any child I have reaches the age of thirty and cannot be used except on behalf of that child. I was aware of Stephen's intentions, he discussed them with me before Waterloo, and I wholeheartedly agree with them. Plus, any man I marry would not be a trustee of that inheritance, and nor would I. Something I totally accept as the correct way to go on. Your brother would receive nothing but me. An extra burden on his outgoings. Now if only I'd known why he was so adamant that he intended to marry me, I could have put him straight. I will do so when I get the chance." She grinned. "A gossip page maybe? With cartoons."

Nicholas chuckled. "I would love to see his face when he is told that. Nevertheless, he is still a menace, and I would swear it would not deter him. He'd expect he would be able to find a way around that."

"I doubt it, Stephen was very thorough. And let's face it, he could have just as easily said the money reverted to the estate."

"True, but I know Gregory. He is like a terrier with a rat."

"Then what do we do? Are you sure he intends to waylay me?"

Nicholas nodded. "So I have been informed. Somehow, yet to be discovered, you would have to put up at the inn for an extra night, and then just after you leave there the following day, he would make his move."

"There is a flaw in your reasoning then. For if I'm not at the inn, won't he know something is amiss?"

"He would if you, or someone who purports to be you, was not said to be staying there. However, if you agree, one Daisy Merton, a rather good actress who your friend Madame Jeanne swears by, will head there and be you. She's waiting in my carriage now."

"Oh, I like it." Isabella clapped her hands. "But…"

Nicholas didn't wait to hear what 'but' she had thought of. He gave her one of his own. "But…whatever the outcome, he'd make sure you would suffer somehow. Not physically, but…"

Lor, those bloody buts.

"In the eyes of the ton?"

"Exactly. You might not think you would care, but you would. If not all the time, the little things would add up and become more important. You know how cruel the tabbies are to those who do not conform to their precepts of polite behaviour. The tenets of the ton are unyielding."

"Then tell me what you suggest," Isabella said in a straightforward manner. The picture he painted was not a pretty one. She might not go out and about in the ton very much, but she would hate not to be given the option. "If you have an idea, please share it, for I'm am out of them. My horses need a rest, my coachmen need a rest, and so do I."

Nicholas leant forward. "Then this is what I suggest…"

Chapter Five

Would she agree with his ideas? Was he asking too much from her? Nicholas waited outwardly with infinite patience, inside with rapidly increasing worry until, after pondering for several minutes, Isabella straightened and tapped one finger on her lips.

Her very kissable lips.

His body tightened as he remembered her taste.

Down, boy. We can but hope, one day…

"Let me get this clear in my mind," she said slowly. "We go to your house. We wed?"

Nicholas nodded.

"Why?"

"So there is no chance Gregory can coerce you into marriage."

"But if I tell him I have no money, why would he still want to wed me?" Isabella asked in a puzzled way. "What would be the point?"

Nicholas shrugged. "He is not the sort to appreciate being thwart…ah, how *stupid* of me." He hit his knee with the palm of his hand, and Isabella jumped. "Of course. Something I have just remembered. I think—think only, mind you—that when he weds, he is given some money for the upkeep of the Abbey. He should have enough without it, our father was well-heeled and careful with his money, but unbeknown to many, the dear duke is a gamester."

"A gamester?" Isabella's eyes were wide and her expression one of astonishment. "That is not well-known, is it? He gambles? Cards? Dice?"

"More in keeping horses to race, that never do any good, eat money, and live a pampered life. He refuses to accept he is not a good judge of horseflesh. Or in where to invest his money. Anything he thinks will make him a quick return, he is all for. He won't listen to anyone. Especially me."

"So is that why you do not talk or…or, well, anything?"

Nicholas shrugged. "Indirectly, I suppose. Dear Gregory wanted me to make him my executor and give him leave to use my money for the upkeep of my lands whist I was away at war. He also thought I should give him a considerable sum to help look after the Abbey. As I know just how much money has been left to him, along with the entail, I declined all of it. I had no intention of coming home to empty coffers. No doubt he hoped I'd be killed as well as so many others at Wa…" He stopped as he remembered who had been killed.

Isabella touched his arm. "You can mention that bloody battle and say his name, it doesn't hurt anymore. I will always love Stephen, but I am not in love with him or his memory. I won't forget him, but I have mourned and had to move on."

Nicholas gulped and swallowed the bile that always hit him when he remembered that sad and sorry day and the senseless loss of life on both sides. "I did try to save him, Isabella, I did, but I couldn't."

"I know, and for that I will always be thankful. More than one person told me how, at great danger to yourself, you crawled to him. You showed you cared. You could do no more. Now, enough, let us look forward. You think this idiotic determination, to put a name to it, of your brother is all down to his profligate lifestyle?"

Nicholas inclined his head. "It seems so. Therefore, as it is illegal to marry your dead brother's wife, if we wed, there is no chance he could find a way to marry you, ever."

"If we wed, I have another question." She cleared her throat. "I, er, will it be a platonic relationship?" she finished in a rush.

He scowled. He had hoped she wouldn't mention that subject. "If you insist."

Isabella nodded. "That is fair enough."

She did not say if that was what she wanted, and Nicholas thought it politic not to ask—yet. "I reserve the right to show you how good we could be together, though," Nicholas said with a grin.

"I reserve the right to decide if I will let you," Isabella riposted. "If, *if* we wed, how and when?"

He tapped his pocket. "I took the liberty of getting a special licence, I believe Gregory also went sometime after me, but I have no idea of the outcome. Nevertheless, I have taken care to warn the vicar I—we—may need his services. In my mind, we do it as soon as possible, and he has agreed and is keeping time free for us."

The words 'just in case' hovered in the air, unspoken but thought, he decided, by both of them.

"So, we wed, and after which we let it be known I am on my way to my house?" Isabella said. "What about Miss Merton? We do not want any harm to come to her."

If he hadn't loved her before, her concern for someone else inveigled into their plot would have done the trick. "She will arrive at the house by a circuitous route, and once you get there you can do the switch. Daisy will stay hidden until we can get her away safely."

"That sounds sensible. You follow—or will you be ahead of me?"

"I think, the best way would be for me watch over you from a short but hidden distance, in case he tries to accost you on the way. Then, once you are safe, we prepare for him to present himself at some point. Remember up until then, he will not know you are spoken for. I will make sure to get there first and hide until my presence is needed. My men and yours will help. I promise you will be safe at all times. One of us will be always be within shouting distance. And armed."

Isabella looked alarmed. "Armed? You think firearms will be needed?"

I have no idea, but I am not prepared to risk your life for lack of foresight."

"Thank you. Nor am I." She leant sideways, and before Nicholas had a chance to blink, a pistol was pointed at him. "It is loaded, but I promise I won't pull the trigger."

She paused and grinned, and put the pistol back in the pocket next to her where she sat. "Yet."

"I am devoutly thankful for that. I will not be so crass as to ask if you can shoot straight. Stephen would not have had it any other way, nor, I suspect, would you."

"Very true. It lives in a secret pocket in the side of the coach. Unless of course it is in *my* pocket or my reticule."

"I will now worry less, but I still reserve the right to worry," Nicholas said frankly, hesitated, then decided to be open and honest. "It may sound far-fetched, but… Ah, Isabella, believe me, I have loved you ever since I first saw you in Lisbon all those years ago."

"What?" she said in a startled manner. "I never realised."

"Of course you didn't," Nicholas replied, as matter-of-fact as he could. "I made sure of that. Plus, you only had eyes for Stephen, which is how it should have been." He took her face between his palms. "Believe me, Isabella, my feelings for you, for both of you, made sure I did try to save him, but I got there too late."

"*Of course* you tried. Good lord, why would I ever think different?" she questioned. "Do not make me angry by thinking any different. I know the type of honourable man you are. Plus, do you *know* how many people told me that?" she demanded. "Described how you, severely injured, crawled to try and aid him? No, *of course* you don't, but I do. Therefore, enough of that."

He smiled. "Yes, my love."

She bit her lip. "I cannot say I love you, but I do have a great fondness for you."

"That is a good place to start," Nicholas said and kissed her softly. To his joy, she responded.

Tentative, and for only a few seconds, but it *was* a definite response. "Many excellent marriages start with fondness, and you have a *great* fondness for me, so we are ahead already."

Isabella laughed. "If you say so."

"I do say so," he assured her. "Well?"

She nodded. "Right, let me see if I have this sorted out in my mind. We let the bugger accost me, and then, with immense glee, I must add, we put paid to his dastardly plans by telling him what has happened. You then offer a one-off lifeline…go to the Indies, and…and what next?"

"We consummate our marriage, enjoy our first Christmas as a married couple, light the Yule log together, live happily ever after?" Nicholas suggested. "Wherever we chose."

She smiled. "I do not believe in fairy tales, my lord. But I do understand what needs to be done. At least in the first instance. I will accompany you to…to where?"

Nicholas realised he hadn't yet divulged where he now called home. "Russets Hall, near Ripon."

Isabella stared and laughed. "You own Russets?"

"Yes," Nicholas said, puzzled by her mirth. "Why?"

"Oh, nothing really. Although I had always wondered who bought it. My house is no more than five or six miles farther north. My godmother left me Bowman Manor."

Nicholas snorted. "Convenient. So do we have a betrothal?"

She bit her lip, and he held his breath.

"We have a betrothal."

"Then let's seal it with a kiss and enable the servants and Daisy do as is needed. We, meanwhile, will head to Russets in my curricle and with luck get there before the snow starts again."

He looked up at the lowering sky. "With that in mind, by your leave, I'll instruct your coachmen to take Daisy to the Red Lion and we will head off. Judging by the weather, I'll forgo the curricle I had intended to use and take the coach my men brought with them. My head groom will be in alt at the opportunity to drive the curricle to Russets. I'd like to get all things sorted as soon as possible, so the sooner we head off the better."

Chapter Six

Nicholas had been as good as his words, and within twenty minutes, Isabella was introduced to Miss Daisy Merton who did indeed have a similar build and from a distance an appearance not unlike that of Isabella, and been assured by Daisy that she would do all that was needed. "Even kneeing him in the balls if need be."

Isabella wouldn't have been human if half of her didn't hope there might be a need for such actions. The two ladies had grinned at each other.

"I trust your judgement," Isabella said with composure she spoiled by laughing. "I just wish I could be a fly on the wall."

"Bloodthirsty women," Nicholas said as he shook Daisy's hand and he and Isabella headed to his coach, and Daisy towards the coach of Isabella. "Remind me never to get on the wrong side of either of you."

Isabella sniggered. "Oh no, the fun is in the surprise."

The closer they got to Nicholas's home, the more anxious Isabella became. Was she doing the right thing? Was she being fair to Nicholas? He said he loved her. What if she could never love him? That the fondness stayed but did not deepen into something more? Would he resent her?

Would *she* resent *him*?

"I can see your mind in turmoil," Nicholas said. "What's wrong?"

Isabella sighed. "I worry."

"About our plans? They will work, I assure you."

"Partly. What if I can never give you what you want? What if you begin to resent the fact, what if…" her voice became softer, huskier, "what if you begin to hate me? Ooft."

Isabella's mind went blank as Nicholas pulled her to him, swept her cloak to one side, and stroked her body with his mouth, and *oh my*, his hands. Her body responded immediately, and his kisses became harder and more insistent. Her nipples hardened, and every inch of her tingled. It might have been several years since she'd been able to enjoy such an arousal, but, she thought hazily, she hadn't forgotten how glorious it was. She moved restlessly whilst his teasing, elegant fingers traced the outline of her breast. Even over her gown his touch affected her.

He has touched my soul.

Isabella moaned. Nicholas pressed her back onto the seat and put one long leg over her body.

Oh my... Totally immersed in the tumultuous feelings she was experiencing, Isabella tugged at his cravat, and when it didn't budge, put her hands under Nicholas's coat and scrabbled at the bottom of his shirt, at the same time he opened the first three buttons of her gown.

The cold air on her heated skin was a wake-up call. She gasped, opened her eyes, and blinked in amazement.

"G...good lord," she stammered.

"What are we doing?"

Heat rushed into her cheeks, and she put her hands to them.

Nicholas pushed his fingers through his hair and grinned. "Well, it's called making love. I touch you, you touch me, we…"

"Oh, you." She grinned back. "I mean here, in a coach, with your men outside and…well, I have no idea where we are, but not far to go, I assume."

Nicholas did the buttons of her gown up again with a deftness that showed he was no stranger to ladies' apparel. He ignored the state of his shirt and cravat. "Hold on, let me check." He put his head out of the window then hastily drew back inside the coach. His eyelashes and hair were speckled white.

"Started to snow, and it's coming down heavily. Luckily we are approaching the village so we only have ten or fifteen minutes to go. Which, I suspect, is just as well." He shook his head, and Isabella ducked.

"Urgh." Drips hit her, and she flinched. They were icy, and she was chilled enough already.

"Oh my goodness, sorry." Nicholas moved away to the far end of the coach and ran his hand over his normally groomed and curly hair. Now it was flat and gleamed with water. "I think we will be happy to arrive. The last half mile could be tricky, but I have every faith in my coachman and horses."

Isabella lifted the side curtain, peered out to look at the ever-increasing snow, which was beginning to obscure the hedges and the darkening sky. It made the scene appear both magical, with icicles sparkling, but also sinister as the landscape disappeared into the gloom. "Are you sure we will get there? It looks as if we are about to hit a drift."

"We have but a few hundred yards before we get to the gates. I'll carry you if need be." He tapped his shoulder. "Over here if necessary."

"Let's hope it isn't necessary then," Isabella said. "It sounds most uncomfortable." To say nothing of inelegant. Goodness knows what would be on show.

"Better uncomfortable than soaking." Nicholas said in a matter-of-fact way. "However, we are about to turn into the drive, and every yard is a yard less to go. Which is a ridiculous thing to say. Talk about stating the obvious." He pointed out of the window. "If it wasn't almost dark, and snowing to impair our view, you would see the house once we pass this clump of trees. As it is, you'll have to wait. And once more that is stating the obvious. Not long now."

"It might all be obvious, but it is also very welcome to hear. How long is the drive?"

Nicholas grimaced. "Just over half a mile, so I will confess I'll be happy *not* to have to carry you."

Isabella giggled, so unlike her normal sensible self that for a moment she was startled. The man managed to bring out facets of herself even *she* didn't know about. "I confess I'll be happy not to be carried. Not over your shoulder at any rate."

"Up the stairs in my arms? To be gently deposited on the bed?" Nicholas asked. He moved closer to her. "Where I can slowly undress you," he whispered. "Until you are naked in my arms. Then I can worship you with my body, come inside you, and…"

"A bit difficult if you're fully clothed," Isabella said breathlessly. His words seeped into her soul and made her yearn to say, 'yes now, soon, and more.' "But it sounds intriguing."

"I'll take that as a positive sign," Nicholas replied. The carriage came to a halt under a welcome portico. "Ah, we are here. Hold fast for a moment until I come round and help you alight." He opened the door on his side and stepped out.

Isabella smoothed her clothing down as he shouted something to an unseen person, and then the door next to her opened.

"Not too deep under cover here, but I'm mighty glad we've arrived. Mrs Thwaite, my housekeeper-cum-cook here, is waiting inside to show you to your room, and her husband, who is my right-hand man on the estate, will carry our luggage inside."

Isabella gasped. "I'd forgotten about luggage. We left mine for Daisy Merton." Was she to spend the next few days in her travelling gown? "That could be awkward."

"Not at all." Nicholas lifted her down, swung her around, and deposited her on the doorstep, just as the door opened to show a smiling, stout, grey-haired lady who was dressed neatly but not fashionably. The housekeeper, Isabella surmised.

"There we are, dry feet. As for luggage? Madame Jeanne turned up trumps. I asked her if she would provide a valise for you to cover all things possible within a sennight or so. She agreed and asked me to tell you it should have everything you need except for food?" He ended his sentence on an upward inflection of query.

Isabella shook out her gown and grinned. "She had already packed one for me at my request, and included some food staples in case I was unable to get any before I arrived at the manor. I couldn't let anyone know I was heading there, well, you know, just in case."

"On which subject I hope to learn more very soon. Once we are in the warm." He took her arm and ushered her inside. "Thwaitey, my love, let me introduce you to my countess-to-be, Lady Isabella. Mrs Thwaite was my nursemaid," he explained to a bemused Isabella.

He buffed Mrs Thwaite soundly on the cheek. "When I outgrew her, she married Thwaite, and they lived at Ashcome, my mama's old home, until I brought here and pleaded with them to save me from slobbishness."

"Give over now, my lord, you've never been a slob. Too fastidious," she added and curtsied to Isabella. "Congratulations, my lady. You've got a fine man there. Not like some that I could mention. Of whom, Master Nick, Thwaite has news."

It enchanted Isabella to see how, once the formalities were over, the lady treated Nicholas. If the atmosphere were always as pleasant and relaxed, she would enjoy living there.

And married? She could but hope she would enjoy that, too.

"If there is news, be it good or bad, we'll be able to assimilate it better once we are warm and dry. Perhaps you could show Isabella to her room, and then once we are ready, we could convene in the small sitting room to catch up. With soup?" Nicholas added. He nodded his thanks to a tall, dark-haired man who stomped by carrying a couple of large cases. Two young lads hefted a trunk between them and followed him.

They headed for the stairs, and the sound of boot steps got softer the nearer they got to the upper floor.

Mrs Thwaite laughed, and her bosom jiggled. "Broth?"

"Thwaitey, you are an angel. Mrs Thwaite makes the best soups and sponge puddings in the area," Nicholas said. "Wins prizes."

"Go on with you, Master Nick." Mrs Thwaite blushed. "You'd eat anything I put in front of you."

"Too true, the food at school was repulsive, in the army not a lot better. Unless I dined with Isabella and Stephen."

Isabella laughed. "Not always. I remember the so-called rabbit stew that in reality was rat." She shuddered. It was perhaps the only time during her sojourn abroad she wished for home. "It was hot, but other than that, I have nothing good to say about it. How the two of you thought you would trick me, I have no idea. It didn't taste at all like rabbit." She rolled her eyes. "There were times when food was hard to come by, but that was the limit. After that, I supervised everything that turned into our dinner."

Mrs Thwaite nodded but had a bemused expression.

"Oh," Isabella said with comprehension. "My late husband and Nicholas were great friends, we entertained him often, especially when I based myself in Lisbon and the pair of them came to the house at every opportunity. I have known him an age, but it is only lately we have become close."

"Ah," Mrs Thwaite said. Her expression cleared. "Now then, isn't that lovely. So, Master Nick, the vicar says he'll do the service at ten in the forenoon, if that's all right with you both. I'll do a nice little wedding breakfast after. And Tom and Billy say they've picked out a good Yule log they'll set up on Christmas Eve and can they bring the greenery for Christmas in a couple of days early to make the place festive for your nuptials?"

Nicholas raised one eyebrow and glanced at Isabella. "Well?"

"Oh, yes please, that would be perfect." She sneezed, and Mrs Thwaite jumped.

"Bless you. Let me show you your room, my lady. The bathwater is ready, and young Effie will have started to unpack for you. If I may be so bold, and if you're in need, she's got the makings of a good little ladies' maid in her. Neat, tidy, unobtrusive, loyal, and eager to learn. You could do a lot worse."

"That's good to know." Isabella followed the older lady in the direction the man had taken. "My, ah, last maid wasn't any of those things. I chose not to inform her of my whereabouts." She would soon be given a reference, her last wages, a bonus, and a Christmas box and told that her services were no longer required.

Nicholas passed them before they reached the bottom stair and took the flight two at a time.

"See you soon." He disappeared down a corridor, whistling as he went.

"Always on the run, even when it's not necessary," Mrs Thwaite said with a fond smile. "Ever since he could walk. Used to annoy his elder brother no end. About whom I will not speak or sully my lips with his name, the…the monster," she said. There was a decided snap in the way she spoke. "Anyroads, here's your sitting room. Master Nick is the other side of your bedchamber."

She opened a door and stood back to let Isabella enter a cosy room decorated in a dusky pink and gold.

To one side of the fireplace, where a bright fire burned and crackled, a chaise and a side table were positioned to make the most of the heat and, Isabella reckoned, the view outside when the long velvet curtains were open.

"The bedchamber is through there." Mrs Thwaite pointed to an open door on the far side of the room. "Your dressing room and the bathing chamber off it. That door to the other side of the fire goes to Master Nick's room. Do you want a key for it?"

Isabella started at the abrupt change of topic. What was the correct answer? She decided to say what she preferred, and if Mrs Thwaite was scandalised, so be it.

"Of course not."

"That's good then. It's been lost for years, but I thought I'd better ask. Now then, here's young Effie to say all's ready for your bath. Ring if you need me." She bustled out, leaving Isabella to face the young girl who stood in the doorway.

"Effie, miss." She bobbed a curtsey, twisted her hands, and appeared scared stiff. "I'm to be your maid if you want me."

Isabella thought she had best make haste to reassure Effie she was no gorgon, and indeed welcomed the fact there was someone to help her.

"I do want you, and if that's my bath ready, Effie, be careful. I might just weep on you in gratitude."

Chapter Seven

Nicholas whistled as he kicked a log with one house-shoe-clad foot, then used a poker to get a larger blaze going. He looked around him with a critical eye but could find no fault with his surroundings.

None of the rooms in the house were overlarge. Russets had originally been a dower house for a large estate several miles away. When he had sold out of the army and discovered it was surplus to that estate's requirements, Nicholas bought it and several hundred acres the owners wanted rid of. It made for a snug and now profitable, small country estate for Nicholas, which was easily manageable by his factor, gamekeeper, and a dozen or so workers outside and a house staff of nine. With a mere six bedrooms and four receptions, it was considered tiny, but it was more than big enough for him. And he hoped, for Isabella.

He wandered over to the sideboard and surveyed the selection of decanters, imaginatively decorated with strands of ivy. A nice touch, due to the season.

Usually he would have a whisky, which arrived at his back door, often with something innocuous as a haunch of venison during the appropriate season. Now he wondered if the smell would put Isabella off?

Off what?

Nicholas smiled to himself. He was overthinking everything again. He poured a tot of whisky and sniffed it with appreciation. Peaty, smoky aromas hit him along with the subtle scent of heather. Perfect with a hearty venison pie. He must make a point of asking if there was any venison left. His stomach rumbled, and his mouth watered at the thought of one of Mrs Thwaite's pies.

The gamey meat he received from a distant cousin was legal, killed at the appropriate time, and hung until needed, but he had long suspected the whisky had not been declared. However, it was good, and Nicholas wasn't going to lose any sleep over the amount of tax the revenue lost. He had a sneaking suspicion that if he had lived near the south coast, the smugglers could have used his barns for their goods without any recriminations.

"If that is whisky, may I join you? Effie showed me where you would be."

He turned to see Isabella standing in the doorway, dressed in a warm, deep-russet down that set her dark hair—styled simply, but well—red lips, deep-blue eyes, and creamy skin off admirably. She wore a paisley shawl around her shoulders and appeared every inch a young lady. Not at all, Nicholas decided, like a dowager. In his mind, the majority of dowagers he knew were like his great aunt. Dour, acerbic, and prone to grumbling about drafts and the youth of the day. None of which could be ascribed to Isabella.

He smiled at her. "Of course you may." Nicholas crossed the room and took her hand to very audaciously turn it over, kiss her palm, then curl her fingers around the spot his lips had touched. "Save it, and remember it."

She sniggered. "For one moment I thought you said savour it."

He inclined his head in appreciation of the sally. "And that. Water or neat?"

Isabella wrinkled her nose. "It has to be with water. If you remember, Ste…" She stopped speaking abruptly. "Oh, tarnation, this is ridiculous. I can't stop saying things that might remind us of him, and do I really want to?"

"I hope not. He is part of both our lives. The only place I hope he doesn't intrude is in the bedroom." He shook his head in mock despair, or he could only hope it was. "That would be somewhat deflating."

Isabella stared at him and then put her hand over her mouth as she laughed behind it. "Oh my…yes, I can see that. Well, no, I can't see it and I hope I won't."

Nicholas raised his eyebrows in query. "The deflation or…?"

Isabella spluttered and then laughed loudly. "Oh…you…Really Nicholas, what next?"

He poured her a good measure of whisky and added water. "I'd better say have a drink. If I went with my other suggestion, and you agreed, we'd be later for dinner and upset Mrs Thwaite. Rubbery Yorkshire puddings and overcooked beef. To say nothing of burnt broth."

"That would never do." Isabella touched her glass to his. "What is it they say over the border, sláinte?"

"Indeed they do. Here, I'll go with the locals and say cheers." He saluted her with his glass. "Tell me what you think. It's, shall we say, special."

She sniffed the liquid and took a sip, rolling it around in her mouth. It was good. Something she had never tasted the likes of before. "Peat?"

"Very good, yes, a peaty malt. Distilled somewhere hidden from the excise men, I imagine."

"Travelled through the night hidden on a wagon of hay?"

"Not in this case, it arrived hidden inside a haunch of venison. My second cousin, Callum, has a way of doing things that although the revenue may not approve, I certainly do. What do you think?"

Isabella swallowed and swirled her drink around. "It's magnificent."

"I'm glad you think so. It gives us one more thing in common."

"A whisky? Would you rescind your offer of marriage if I said I hated it?" Isabella asked quizzically. "I would have thought you would decide that if I declined to drink it, then it would be all the more for you."

"Hmm…now you have made me wonder…" He laughed and ducked out of the way of her mock punch. "Don't worry, you matter more than a mutual appreciation of whisky, but I am glad you enjoy it. Brandy next?"

"Now there you have me. I enjoy rum and sherry, but I have never managed to drink brandy without shuddering, not even watered down."

"Another thing in common," Nicholas said. "I don't shudder but I never choose it in preference over anything else."

There was the sound of a gong from outside the room, and Nicholas held out his arm. "Shall we? I suspect Mrs T will have pulled out all the stops, especially as we have thwarted her chances of preparing a large wedding breakfast."

Isabella put her arm on his and sighed. "What else can we do?"

"Nothing now, but hopefully later when the weather is better, we can have a celebration. She can pull out all the stops for us then."

"Then shall we tell her?" Isabella suggested. "I think she would appreciate it, and I can also reassure her that Effie is perfect for me. I will be happy to appoint her my new ladies' maid. How providential I decided that Bessie, the maid I had in London, was not the sort of person I wanted near me. I suspect she was the one who made sure my whereabouts were conveyed to your brother. My trusted staff agreed with me. Nevertheless, she is still employed for now, as I didn't think it sensible to show my suspicions."

"Once we are married she can be let go."

"That's true. Oh look, how lovely."

They had entered the dining room, where crystal sparkled and another fire burned bright and welcoming in a large ornate grate. Candles set at either end of the mantel and in two candelabras, on the sideboard and one on the table, gave the room a romantic, intimate air.

Christmas greenery already decorated the mantel and around the framed pictures on the walls. Winter roses were arranged in a wide-necked vase set between two floor-to-ceiling, curtained windows, and ivy twined around the vases and the bottom of the candelabras. Isabella fell in love with the room as soon as she saw it.

And Nicholas? Well, if she were honest, she was also well on the way to loving him.

He stood to one side and watched her wander around and take her fill. A smile played over his lips.

Did he like what he saw?

A shadow from behind him showed Mrs Thwaite, and Tom, her son, standing holding tureens and plates. None of them moved until Isabella turned in their direction and put her hand to her throat.

"Oh, ohh my, I am *so* sorry. I was struck by the sheer perfection of this room and forgot we were here because the gong had sounded. I haven't spoiled anything, have I?"

"Deary me, no, my lady," Mrs Thwaite said with a blatant disregard for the truth. Tom winced.

It appeared his mother lied with aplomb.

"It'll keep."

"But not for long, I daresay," Isabella replied with a smile. "So we will seat ourselves immediately." She moved to the table and sat, even before Nicholas could help her. Thank goodness his place was easily spotted by the tankard of ale placed to one side next to a carving knife and fork. The chairs were no help, they were identical and the table round, no head or foot. It was obvious to see this room was not used for entertaining.

For which she was thankful. She liked the idea of a room just for them to use.

"We'll serve ourselves, Mrs T," Nicholas said.

That lady nodded and put the contents of the trays onto the table.

"Once we've eaten," Nicholas added, "we can all convene in the sitting room and discuss what you know, what we know, and what we're going to do."

Mrs Thwaite nodded. "There's a curd tart for after, even though it's not the season. Enjoy your dinners." She bustled out followed by Tom.

Isabella surveyed the table. "There's enough here to feed a family of seven for a sennight. We will never eat all that."

"We're not meant to," Nicholas said. "We eat what we can, as do the staff who will have the same fare. I decreed that as an absolute when I first bought the place. So we eat, the staff eat at the same time, and anything that is left is distributed to the rest of the estate workers and then the village. The vicar oversees that for me."

"Oh, what a good idea." That was a deed to remember.

"But, it doesn't mean you have to stint yourself and not eat as much as you want or need," Nicholas pointed out. "Mrs T knows to the last slice of bread or Yorkshire pudding how much extra is needed."

Chapter Eight

"I couldn't have eaten another thing," Isabella declared when she and Nicholas settled themselves side by side on a long sofa and waited for Mrs Thwaite and the others to arrive. She nursed a glass of port and twirled the goblet in her hands before sipping. The glow of the fire highlighted the golden glint in her hair and made her eyes darker, full of secrets and mystery.

A smile played over her full and sensual lips. She licked the port from them, and not for the first time, Nicolas was struck how innocently provocative that gesture was.

He experienced the now familiar tension of arousal that hit him whenever she smiled at him, and his body—and mind—responded. If only they could forget everything and everyone else, go upstairs, and enjoy the delights of each other's bodies. To touch caress and share feelings, sensations, and sate themselves. Which brought Nicholas's thoughts up short. He knew nothing about Isabella's likes and dislikes, or indeed if she enjoyed making love. What if she was one of those women who submitted because she had been told that was the way of their world, but didn't connect mentally with her lover or enjoy all the things they could do together? What a depressing thought.

The knock on the door brought his introspection to a stop, which was probably a good thing. He could do nothing about how Isabella felt, or thought, until they had a chance to talk alone. Meanwhile, there were other more pressing things to discuss.

"Yes, we're ready, come on in."

Mrs Thwaite, her husband and son, and the rest of the staff filed in and ranged themselves in front of Nicholas and Isabella. Nicholas stood and offered his chair to Mrs Thwaite who shook her head.

"Go on with you, Master Nick, that's not the done thing."

"It is here," Nicholas said firmly. "I cannot sit whilst a lady stands."

Mrs Thwaite went red with pleasure and, flustered, sat down in a hurry. She smoothed her skirts and straightened her sleeves.

Isabella leant towards her. "Thank you," she whispered. "Or I would have felt the need to stand, and my feet hurt."

"Bless you, my lady. It feels strange, but then Master Nick has always had a sense of right and a mind of his own."

Nicholas overheard the exchange and bit back a grin. Who else's mind *would* he have? He turned his thoughts to the matter in hand.

"That's better." Nicholas stood to one side so he could see everyone. "So what do we know about my dear brother and his antics?"

"It seems His Grace found out where…" Thwaite coughed. "I'm sorry, Master…er, my lord, I'm a bit flummoxed as to what to call the dowager, er, my lady."

"My lady is perfect," Isabella said before Nicholas could reply. "I don't think I could pass myself of as Miss Isabella these days."

Thank you," Thwaite said gratefully. "Then it seems His Grace has discovered where my lady's house is, and as you thought, intended to accost her after she left the last inn but before she arrived at her house. The, ah..." He cleared his throat delicately. "Er, young lady you engaged to act as my lady is safely ensconced in, and His Grace not far away. Young Tom visited the inn earlier and found out that two of His Grace's horses have been stabled at The Three Horse Shoes whilst he stays at The Greyhound."

"The coachmen are at the Horse Shoes," Tom said. "His Grace has his man with him. It seems he asked to be woken early. According to a friend of mine, who works as a chambermaid at The Three Horse Shoes, My Lady, The Dowager Duchess, is keeping to her room. It seems so far all is going to plan, except it is thought His Grace will make his move tomorrow, not the day after. No reason as to why has come to anyone's ears. Miss Merton has been made aware and says she will go for her walk as you arranged and be vigilant."

"We've got a guard for her set up nice and tight," Thwaite said. "And Billy, and Young Sim Smithers, the blacksmith, are keeping an eye over yonder. We'll be well warned of whatever goes down."

"Do you really think something is likely to…" Isabella paused, "go down?"

"No," Nicholas said bluntly. "But if there was one thing the army taught me, it was prepare for the worst. So a guard here, plus one over Daisy and my bloody brother, we must have." He shook hands with each of the staff in the room. "We will marry and then set out to be ready to accost Gregory as he waylays Daisy. She knows not to leave the inn before noon. I thank you for all your hard work. If it could be arranged for as many of you as possible to be at the church in the morning, then I would be happy to see you there."

"We would." Isabella stood next to Nicholas. "I feel part of this family already. To have you there would be special."

"Then we'll see what we can do," Mrs Thwaite said. "As long as all is right and tight and safe for you both here, I'll be there. And now I best go rescue my cake that's in the oven, if that's all right."

Nicholas gave an exaggerated sniff. "Of course, can I smell burning?"

"You better not." Mrs Thwaite left the room in a hurry, and the others followed at a more regular pace. "Or you'll be on bread and gruel for your wedding celebrations," she called over her shoulder.

"I doubt it," Nicholas said, as once more he and Isabella were alone. "According to Thwaite, he got told it was leftovers for bait—that's a snack—as she was too busy sorting tomorrow out to make cakes for 'lowance time." He smiled, and Isabella burst out laughing. "So, no reneging, my dear, Mrs Thwaite would never forgive us."

"Oh, I couldn't let that happen," Isabella said with a gurgle that enchanted him. "That is a very good reason to wed."

Nicholas put his elbow on the mantel and stared at the fire for a few seconds without speaking. There was a soft swish of velvet skirts when Isabella joined him and leant on his side.

"What is wrong?" she asked softly. "If you wish to withdraw your offer, it's not too late. I will be fine."

"To be frank, that is what worries me," Nicholas said. He put his arm around her and turned so they faced each other. "Do you really want to marry me? Me as I am? Me because you have a fondness for me, not just because I'm convenient? If it is the latter, well, we will survive, but if it is more than that, I would like to know." He held his breath. "Or even if you ever think there might be a chance you could love me."

Isabella stared at the man in front of her and realised just how unfair she had been. Nicholas had done all the giving, and she had taken it gladly with no thought of his feelings, or indeed any reciprocation.

"I think, my lord," she said and grinned before she outlined his lips with her finger. She'd enjoyed him doing it to her, so why should the enjoyment not be mutual? "I think *you* overthink. So much indeed, that I worry you might not agree to my request." She tilted her head to one side in query. "Or is it a plea, I wonder? Perhaps it is both."

Nicholas drew her finger into his mouth and suckled, hard.

Isabella gasped.

"Ni…ch…olas."

He lifted his head and did the raised eyebrow query expression she loved. "Yes?"

"You…"

"I?"

He wasn't going to help her. Isabella slowly undid his waistcoat buttons and then unpinned the simple gold bar in his cravat. "I think you are overdressed, my lord." She took a deep breath and unwound the yard of cloth. Grasped both his hands and twisted the material around his wrists. "I hope you have more cravats, I fear this one may soon appear beyond redemption."

"I have plenty." He stood and waited.

Only by his heightened colour and the rapid beat of the pulse at the base of his throat could she tell he was affected.

Please let it be in a positive way.

"Ah, good." Isabella paused and then decided to be honest, open, and say what she wanted. "Oh, tarnation, my lord. I think you better take me to bed and make me yours. Then you'll see just how much I want you as you and no one else."

Now she understood the expression, even the air stood still.

Chapter Nine

If it were a dream, then she'd happily stay in it forever. Never open her eyes, just absorb all those beautiful feelings and sensations that had both bombarded her and crept up on her.

Isabella stretched her arms in the air, enervated, languid, and sated. She brought them down to hit something.

It uttered a mumph… "What…?"

She opened her eyes in a hurry.

Nicholas was in the process of rolling over to pin her beneath him. "There's better ways of waking me, my love."

Isabella wriggled. One hard part of his anatomy dug into her belly. "I think part of you is well awake already," she said dryly and slithered up a little so his staff was almost inside her. "I think he wants to play." *Argh, how coy.*

"I think so as well." Nicholas inched into her with erotic and excruciating unhurried care. "He wants to be reassured last night wasn't a dream." He began to move in a slow and sensual rhythm, which Isabella matched eagerly.

"So do I," she said breathlessly. The tempo increased and so did her arousal. "I remember this, though." She stroked his back and kneaded his buttocks.

Nicholas groaned. "Oh, so do I. How about this."

He bent his head and nipped one of her nipples with his teeth, none too gently. Enough to sting, harden, and send a sharp pleasure-pain of awareness through her. Isabella arched into him, gasped, and screamed. Her climax hit her deep and fast, way before she had registered she was on the cusp.

Her release acted like a sign to Nicholas. He shuddered, shook, pushed harder and faster, then stiffened before he shouted his completion. Warmth flooded her as he slumped boneless onto her body, his breath harsh in her ear.

"It wasn't a dream," Nicholas said several minutes later, when at last he could speak coherently. "I'm so glad about that."

Isabella smiled and kissed his neck. "As am I. I ache, am happily weary, and hope you now accept how much I want you."

He nodded. "Good."

"In fact," Isabella said, "I could stay in bed with you all day."

To his disappointment, she put on her dressing gown over her nakedness—her nightrail was somewhere, but he had no idea where. Why hadn't he hidden the dressing gown?

"But I think I'd better not." She tied the belt round her waist.

"A pity. I could with you as well. But we have a wedding to go to."

She grinned. "I am so looking forward to the vicar asking me if I will love, honour, and obey. The first two I will do with all my heart." She paused and made a tiny erotic click with her tongue. "I give you fair warning, my love, I may well cross my fingers when I say obey and add under my breath, the proviso, 'when it is sensible to do so'."

Nicholas laughed. "I expect nothing less." He sobered. "Your love? Am I? Are you sure?"

"Oh yes, I am certain. It crept up on me, and then, there I was, in love with the man I yearn to marry. In f…" She stopped speaking and raised one eyebrow in query. A commotion could be heard from outside. "What on earth?"

Nicholas sprang out of bed, pulled his banyan over his head, and drew back the curtains so vigorously the rings that held them in place jangled. "No idea, but perhaps we better get dressed and find out. I'll nip into my dressing room and see you in your sitting room as soon as possible. Can you manage?"

Isabella looked at her reflection in the mirror. Rat's nest hair, an expression of well-loved satisfaction, and some tell-tale red marks on her neck. "Of course I can." *I hope.* She hurried to the armoire, picked a gown that needed no help to do up, and checked how much water there was in the ewer. Enough, even if it was cold. She hurried through her ablutions and dressed. Her hair would be hardest, but a quick brush, and she plaited it into a simple coronet. It would have to do.

She arrived at the sitting room through one doorway, just as Nicholas entered via another and there was a knock at the door that led to the corridor.

Nicholas nodded to her. "Good timing. Let's see what's next." He walked to the door and opened it.

Thwaite stood there with a horrified expression.

"It's His Grace," she said. "Here with that Daisy Merton. They insist they see both of you immediately. Important, His Grace said, and he added not to worry. Ha, wouldn't trust him as far as our Tom could throw him, and he's no bowler. Don't you worry nowt, though, neither of you, we're all armed now, my lord, even our Libby, and have your backs."

"Armed?" Nicholas said, apprehensive at the thought of so many guns in the hands of worried or scared people. "Be careful, for God's sake, and don't go shooting anyone without good reason. We'll come down. Where have you put them?"

"In the study, with Billy outside the window and our Tom at the door keeping an eye on them."

Too zealous? Nicholas had no idea and no intention of saying so. "Thank you. Could you ask Libby to arrange refreshments? We're on our way."

He waited until Thwaite had gone and turned to Isabella.

"Are you armed?"

"I will be, in one moment." She disappeared into her dressing room and was back almost before he'd found his pistol, checked it was loaded, and put it in his pocket.

"Ready?"

"Ready."

He took her hand as much for his sake as hers. "Then let's go."

The sight before them as they entered the study could have been farcical if not so serious.

Tom stood, arms crossed, in front of the open study door, and Billy could be seen through the window.

His Grace, the Duke of Ancaster, dressed as precise as ever, sat calmly on a settee sipping ale. Beside him Daisy Merton, clothed in one of the gowns Madame Jeanne had given to Isabella, did the same.

It suited her.

Neither looked murderous or full of ill intent. If anything, they appeared happy and content.

"So to what do we owe this honour?" Nicholas drawled.

"To tell you that as of yesterday, Miss Merton agreed to be my duchess," his brother replied. "We, er, met and I realised I knew her from long ago. When she lived on our estate with her parents who worked for Papa. She saw me, and to tell the truth…"

"I hit him over the head with my umbrella and asked him what he thought he was playing at," Daisy said. "Told him what I thought of him and his holier than thou, he was right, 'give no consideration to anyone else's views or feelings' attitude."

The duke smiled, not at all how Nicholas had expected him to react.

Is this really my brother?

"The upshot being, I explained I needed to marry to release some capital."

"I put him straight about a few things," Daisy said in a fond voice. "Told him it was not acceptable that he, the bugger, thought to coerce Lady Isabella into marrying him. Rubbish, when anyone could have told him you two were meant for each other. Nigh on criminal it would have been, and that sort of behaviour wasn't worthy of him."

Gregory nodded ruefully and fingered the top of his head. "Luckily the bruise was a minor one. So I said in that case maybe she'd like to marry me instead."

"And I said yes." Daisy giggled. "You always love your first, don't you? Him who does the deflowering, if he does it well, holds a special place in your heart. My Gregory certainly has that."

Gregory reddened as Isabella laughed and Nicholas howled.

"Yes, well, maybe a tad too much information, my love," Gregory said in a fond tone.

"Rubbish," Daisy said briskly but with a laughing glint in her eye. "We're all adults and know what the gooseberry bush is like." She winked. "Don't we, my lady."

"Oh yes. How v-very true," Isabella stuttered. "Do go on, both of you."

Gregory inclined his head. "Therefore, I wish to apologise to you both and say that you do not need to have any worries about me and my unpleasant, and unwelcome advances, my lady, or my unpleasant attitude. I hope in time we can become friends, or at least comfortable in each other's company. It appears your marriage is not necessary any more."

"Oh yes it is," Nicholas and Isabella said together.

"For as you said," Isabella remarked with a wicked glance in Nicholas' direction, "you never forget he who deflowered you. Even if he then took a good ten or so years more to make any move, even once the mitigating circumstances were no more."

Nicholas gave her a hug, which she returned with fervour. "Well, they're removed now, so...?"

"So we have a wedding to attend," Isabella said. "And now we have two more witnesses to hear us say 'I do'."

Fairy Dust Wishes

Cassie O'Brien

'*Ding-dong merrily on high. In heaven the bells are ringing…*'

The opening lines of the carol reverberated through the speaker recessed in the ceiling above my head for the sixth time that day, which, loving everything about Christmas as I did, bothered me not at all. My colleague stood alongside me behind the perfumery counter of Robins and Son—purveyors of fine goods since eighteen-ninety-nine—felt somewhat differently. Her face frozen in the rigor mortis of pleasantness, our floor supervisor, Felicity, insisted on keeping the customers sweet, her mouth barely moving as she hissed through gritted teeth.

"For pity's sake. Give it a bleedin' rest, will you? If I never hear bloody ding-dong again, it'll be too soon."

I grinned. I had some sympathy for her plight. There were still four shopping days to go before the store closed on Christmas Eve, and since the beginning of December the same ten songs had played over and over on a continuous loop—the store's antiquated eight-track sound system only possessing one cartridge of festive tracks.

"Never mind, Sarah. Slade's *Merry Christmas Everyone* is up next."

Her voice was low enough to reach my ears only. "And they can fuck right off and do one, too."

My laugh nearly snorted down my nose, but I managed to hold it back when an elderly white-haired gentleman approached the counter and I asked, "Can I help you, sir?"

He looked at the profusion of parfums, eau de toilette, and mist sprays displayed before him with a bewildered expression. "Ah…the wife…she likes light and flowery, I think."

I picked up a wodge of test strips and made my way to his side of the counter with a smile. "Shall we try some of the samples and see if you recognise her favourite scent or something similar to it?"

Relief lit his eyes. "That would helpful if you can spare the time? The store is very busy."

I gave him the ghost of a wink. "It would be nothing but a pleasure to step away from the hurly-burly for a while, sir. We'll find her something lovely, I'm sure."

Felicity gave me a nod of approval for the sleekness of my sales technique, which although appreciated, wasn't necessary. To help someone discover a Christmas gift, which I pictured being unwrapped with surprised happiness, was more a pleasure than a business transaction to me.

Given his age, I led him away from the sweeter fragrances with their underlying notes of bubble gum and candy floss so beloved by the under twenty-fives and towards the perfumes comprised of floral notes created by Chanel, Dior, and Givenchy.

Many squirts and sniffs later, he stroked his silver beard. "Yes, that's the one. How much is it, please?"

I told him, and his face fell.

"Well, thank you for your help. I'll think it over."

"The eau de toilette is ten pounds less," I offered.

He thought for a moment then shook his head. "Close but not quite near enough to what I have to spend. Now, I'd best get back to the grotto. My lunch break's over."

His face seemed somewhat familiar, and it dawned on me. "You're our Santa this year? In the toy department on floor two?"

He nodded. "But off-duty in mufti at the moment. After all, no one wants to see Mr Claus chomping on a Maccie D's or using the Gent's loos."

I smiled. "Then why not use your staff discount? That'll knock another twenty percent off the price."

He shrugged. "Temporary staff don't get a discount card."

It had been so many years since I'd been put on the permanent payroll, I'd forgotten that, and I couldn't bear the disappointment on his face. "Then I'll use mine and buy it for you. I could bring the perfume to the staff canteen and you can pay me back?"

"You would spend your own money and trust me to do that?"

I looked into his eyes of periwinkle blue, and his honesty twinkled back at me in a way that left me with no doubts. "Of course. If you can't put your faith in Santa, I don't who you can."

He chuckled then peered at the name embroidered on the pocket of my blouse. "Then, thank you, Ms. Megan Jones. I accept. If you tell me when your afternoon tea break is, I will take mine at the same time."

"I'm late rota today—so half past three."

He glanced at my left hand, bare of any rings. "I'll see you there, miss. You'll have no trouble spotting me. I'll be wearing my ho-ho-ho suit—a twenty-minute interlude to grab a cuppa is not enough time to change out of it."

I picked up a cellophane-wrapped sealed box of his choice from the display. "See you later, Mr Claus."

He glanced over his shoulder as he turned away. "If I can't leave the grotto on time, look out for an elf. He'll be dressed for the part. You won't be able to mistake him."

I nodded and rang his purchase through the till, applying my own discount code. The bill would be deducted from my wages at the end of the month, but to all intents and purposes it was paid for, so I giftwrapped it in the fanciest paper I could find and tucked it out of sight beneath the countertop.

Sarah nudged my arm and whispered, "What was that about?"

I muttered. "He's our Santa, but seasonal workers don't get staff discount, so I bought it for him with mine."

She raised her eyes heavenward. "Megan, you are such a sucker for a sob story!"

I shook my head. "No. He'll pay me back in the canteen at tea break this afternoon."

Sarah frowned. "I hope so. I know you've already spent your month-end wages on pressies to take home."

There was no time for more, and the afternoon sped by. In the run-up to Christmas, our section was always busy, mainly with men suddenly remembering they needed to purchase a gift for their wife or lover, mother or sister. Felicity released us at twenty to four when Amber and Jess sauntered back from their break.

"Sorry," Jess apologised without meaning it. "The store's that rammed it took us a while to push through the crowds."

Sarah gave her the fakest smile I'd seen in years. "Thanks for the warning, and no worries. It'll probably take us twice as long to get back from ours."

I plucked the wrapped gift from beneath the counter. *I Wish It Could Be Christmas Everyday*, belted out from the speakers as we left the shop floor and made our way up the back stairs to the staff canteen. Mr Claus sat at a table on the far side of the room, but I nearly tripped over my own feet when I saw the man sitting beside him.

He wasn't short, although not overly tall as befitted an elf, and his waves of chestnut hair were swept back from his brow and captured by a leather thong at the nape of his neck — but it was his shoulders and torso tightly encased in a belted green tunic that caused me to hiccup.

'Oh my!'

Many hours of gym work must have been involved.

Sarah's eyes followed my gaze as she picked up a tray. "Bloody hell! The store's budget doesn't normally stretch to employing proper Guild actors, does it? I swear that one's just walked off the set of *Lord of the Rings*."

I followed her to the serving hatch, grabbed a mince pie from the display, and added it to the tray. "Santa's looking pretty authentic in his ho-ho-ho suit, too. Robins and Son must have really pushed the boat out this year. I wonder how much they're charging for the grotto?"

She plonked a large square of chocolate fudge cake beside my pie. "Whatever it is, it I bet it's expensive."

The lady behind the hatch handed us two mugs of tea to my huffed, "Then I hope the kids queuing up are receiving more than a cheap painting book and a pack of wax crayons for their hour-long wait."

The canteen was packed with all the regular staff plus the additional seasonal workers taken on to rake in the cash during the lucrative Festive Season that ensured an old-fashioned department store like ours would survive for another year. There wasn't a table anywhere near Mr Claus not fully occupied, so I waved to catch his eye then set our tray down on a table for four that only had Ronnie and Dave from Men's Shoes sitting to one side of it.

Dave swallowed his mouthful of Christmas cake. "All right girls? Bloody hectic, isn't it? Shoes and Lingerie are going for a pint at the Rose and Crown after work. You lot from Perfume up for it?"

Sarah sipped her tea. "Yeah, why not. I've got nothing to rush home for. What about you, Megan?"

My heart squeezed its habitual yearning that one day I would share my love of Christmas with someone special, and I answered, "Sure. My flatmate's out on her office shindig tonight, and I'm not driving until Christmas Eve."

"You're working right up until the last knockings, too?" Ronnie asked glumly.

I nodded. "Yeah. I got a half-day holiday on Christmas Eve last year, so I'm on rota until the shop closes at five."

Sarah tutted. "You've got a two-hundred-mile drive to get home, Megan. I'd throw a sickie."

"And that's why if *either* of you are absent from work on the twenty-fourth, you will receive a first-strike, written, disciplinary warning." Unnoticed, Felicity had glided up to the table behind us.

Sarah silently mouthed a very rude word.

I met Felicity's eyes. "I think you'll find mine and Sarah's absence records are exemplary if you check. Even at this time of year."

She sniffed. "They had better be."

I watched her walk away and felt the touch of a hand on my shoulder. I glanced up and became lost in two pools of emerald green fringed with long lashes that matched the colouring of his hair. My breath caught in the back of my throat as I gazed at the most kissable lips I'd ever seen. "Megan? Santa says he owes you forty pounds?"

My lungs experienced a sudden lack of oxygen that made my voice squawk. "I can wait if it's a problem."

Sarah kicked my shin. "No, you can't. You bought your nephews that Nintendo game they wanted yesterday. Remember?"

I blushed.

The elf smiled and held out two twenty-pound notes. "He wouldn't want you to."

I took them and swallowed hard. He gazed into my eyes as if we were the only two people in the room.

"And you, Megan. What is it you want for Christmas?" he asked.

My head rang with my silent reply. *'A bough of mistletoe, and you would do nicely, thanks.'*

He glanced towards the ceiling as if he'd heard my answer and expected the greenery to be dangling above us, then smiled. "A kiss to build a dream on…"

Felicity clapping her hands loudly broke the spell. "Perfume, Toiletries, Beauty…back to work."

I stood and handed him the wrapped gift for Santa's wife. "I hope Mrs Claus likes it."

"I'm sure she will."

I turned away, and it occurred to me I hadn't asked his name. But he must have been tardier than me returning to work after his break and left the canteen at quite a run, for there was no sign of him. I spent the rest of the afternoon kicking myself for being too tongue-tied as not to think of inviting him to the pub.

The bar was packed when we pushed through its doors after work. Laughter accompanied by the warm buzz of conversation filled the space, and Dave waved to attract our attention. I followed Sarah as she made her way through the throng to reach him. He and Ronnie had a pint each in hand. A bottle in an ice bucket with two empty glasses stood on the table beside them.

Dave grinned. "We thought Felicity might not excuse you a minute before she had to, so we got you one in."

Sarah picked up the bottle. "Ooh, rosé Prosecco. I like that."

Dave gazed at her waves of long red hair, and his eyes softened. "Yeah. I hoped you might."

I grinned, and Ronnie raised his eyes heavenward. Neither Sarah nor Dave noticed him pouring pink fizzy wine into her glass. We sat.

Ronnie did the same for me then toasted me with his pint. "I'm only here for a couple of beers. Deanne's taken the kids to her mum's for their tea, and I said I'd be home by bath time."

I knew he had two young children, a boy and a girl. "Are they excited? I bet they are. My nephews are that hyped they're driving my brother mad. I can't wait to see them unwrap their presents on the big day."

He smiled. "They are, and I can't either. You haven't got any of your own?"

My heart did its weird clenching thing, but I ignored it and shrugged. "Unfortunately not. Mr Right hasn't come along yet."

He sipped his beer and answered comfortingly, "You're a really nice girl. I'm sure he will."

The words ricocheted through my mind, although I didn't voice them. *I wish he'd get a move on then. I'm not a girl. I'm nearly bloody thirty!* Instead, I smiled as I always did, then changed the subject to a happier one. "One day perhaps, but never mind that. I've bought my nephews the latest Mario game for their Nintendo Switch. What are your kids hoping for?"

I passed a very pleasant half hour chatting to him, but when our glasses were empty, we left Sarah and Dave to it, wished each other goodnight, and went our separate ways. In lieu of all the calories I knew I would eat over Christmas at my parents' house, I didn't call into the kebab shop on my way home, although my stomach rumbled at the savoury smell when I walked past it. I let myself in, and my flat was empty of my house-share, Carly. I brewed a coffee and sat on the sofa with the tree lit but the overhead lights out. This time last year I had thought my future would be on a different path to how it had turned out.

Lee and I had been dating for nearly two years. He'd met my family and me his. We stayed over at each other's places every other night. I'd been half hoping to find a sparkly engagement ring under the Christmas tree, but as chilly November arrived, what I got instead was the big heave-ho—the girl he'd longed to be with since he was about twelve had finally noticed his existence. I was sad but not miffed. He let me down gently, but the joy in his eyes when he said her name told me that to try and hold on to him would only lead to unhappiness all round. He married Gemma seven months later, and their happiness reflected in the Facebook pics of the occasion showed he'd made the right choice.

It wasn't a memory to make me smile, but still I did at the sight of my sparkling Christmas tree and the wrapped gifts beneath it. Each had been chosen with care, and I enjoyed seeing them on view until the day I packed them into the boot of my car and drove home for Christmas. My parents would have decorated the house to within an inch of its life. My brother, his wife, and my two nephews, would arrive by lunchtime on Christmas Eve—my grandparents would have been ensconced for at least a week. There would be much laughter. Our family liked and loved each other, and none of us lived that close that to spend the holidays in each other's company would be a burden. Three more days. I couldn't wait!

The crunch of a key turning in the front door sounded, so I sat straighter and finished my coffee. Carly walked into the sitting room with a big grin on her face and a polystyrene takeout box in each hand. The luscious smell of lamb hit my nostrils, and my belly growled its demand to be fed even as I objected. "You cowbag! No kebabs this week, I said."

She laughed and wafted the containers of hot food under my nose. "Yeah, yeah. Extra jalapenos and chilli sauce. Tell me you don't want it?"

My mouth watering, I snatched one. "I'm going to be the size of a bloody house come New Year."

She giggled and plonked herself beside me. "You and me both, babe. Still, we've got four or five months afterwards to get our bikini bods back in shape."

The following day, I arrived at work and found Sarah already in position behind the counter. The store was that frantic from the time the doors opened I didn't have chance to ask her how her evening had gone after I'd left, but her humming along to the festive tracks she'd previously despised gave me a clue.

She grabbed my arm when Felicity allowed us to go to the canteen for our morning coffee break. "Come on. Let's get up there."

Nothing loath, in the hope of seeing a tightly fitting green tunic, I sped after her. Her hopes were fulfilled, mine were not. Dave, sitting at a table alongside Ronnie, waved. Robins and Son's more habitual Santa was perched on a stool wearing his fake beard and somewhat threadbare red suit with no sign of an elf.

I pushed Sarah in Dave's direction. "Get over there. I'll get the coffees."

I picked up two steaming frothy mugs once I'd been served and paused at Santa's table. "Hey, Bob. I thought you weren't working this year? There was a different guy in the grotto yesterday."

He wiped a dribble of coffee from the side of his mouth with a paper serviette. "Yeah. I 'ad a bit of a problem wiv my teeth. Me top set of dentures broke a couple of days into this year's stint. Can't talk to the kiddies all gummy like, so the management got a stand-in till they were fixed. He was a good guy, though. Told the company to make up my statutory sick pay to what I'd normally earn, and he'd take a lower amount 'cos it was a gig he'd always fancied doing."

It hit me like a ton of bricks. *That's why he couldn't afford the perfume. I'm so glad I used my staff discount.*

I smiled. "Yeah. He seemed really nice."

Bob nodded. "From what I heard, his costume was top-notch, same as the bloke working with him. I reckon they're a pair of pro actors getting a few shifts in so they know what to expect from the kids when this year's pantomime opens at the Festival Theatre on Christmas Eve."

I made a mental note to book a ticket for New Year once I returned from my parents' if that was the case, then asked, "Um, did you hear what their real names are?"

Bob shrugged. "I never heard Santa called anything other than that, but Susie told me his sidekick is called Gethin."

I smiled, walked away, and my heart sank. Susie—the beautiful long-limbed blonde who manned the counter on Toys. I cancelled the fictional theatre ticket in my head. A five-foot-three, plumpish brunette didn't stand a chance.

Sarah barely noticed me putting her coffee in front of her.

Ronnie winked at me. "They're oblivious, I'm afraid."

I agreed. "I think you're right, although they've worked here together for the last year or so. What do you reckon took them so long?"

He sipped his coffee. "Timing. Opportunity. Sometimes it takes a while, sometimes its quicker.

My mate and his wife pratted around for three years before they started dating, but I knew within a few hours of meeting Deanna, she was the one for me. Their relationship isn't any stronger because they took their time, ours isn't flimsier because it took off from day one."

I wished I could relate to either scenario, but for however long or short a time I'd dated someone, that particular end result had never come my way.

Ronnie's phone bleeped, and he nudged Dave. "Come on, mate. That's the alarm. Coffee break's over. Back to work."

Dave, with some reluctance, set his mug on the table. They stood. "See you later, girls."

We nodded. I sipped my coffee. Sarah's gaze never left Dave as he exited the canteen.

The door swung shut behind him, and I knocked her knee with mine. "So…?"

She smirked and teased, "So, what?"

I huffed theatrically. "So, what happened after I left the bar last night?"

She gave in and grinned. "So, Dave might have come back to mine and might not have left until this morning."

I laughed. "It took you two enough time to get it together."

"I always liked him and him me, but I was going out with Greg, and he was engaged to that Jenny until she broke it off to go off backpacking around the world with her mate."

Felicity cleared her throat loudly behind us.

Sarah scraped her chair back and stood. "Yeah, yeah. We get the message."

I followed her through the canteen, and she glanced at Bob.

"I thought we had a new Santa this year?" Sarah asked.

"Temporary cover while Bob was off sick, but he's back now," I told her.

She shrugged. "Ah, well…"

The rest of the morning passed in a whirl, and at one, Felicity signalled for us to take our lunch break, but before I could trot after Sarah to the canteen, Carly appeared at the counter, white-faced and wearing totally out-of-season sunglasses.

She looked like she might vomit imminently and announced, "Oh God, I need grease inside me to mop up last night's alcohol. Take me to Archie's and feed me a bacon, sausage, and fried egg sarnie?"

I laughed. "Yep, along with a giant-sized mug of black coffee from the state of you."

She sighed. "Yes, please."

I took Carly's hand, towed her behind me out of the store, and pushed open the door to Archie's café five minutes later. Given the time of year it was packed, but I saw a table for two near the takeout till. I pulled out a chair for her to sit on, and she grumbled.

"I hate this spot. No wonder it's free with everyone shoving past it after they've collected their containers of food to go."

I picked up the menu. "We can thank our lucky stars we've got somewhere to sit at all. The place is crammed with shoppers at this time of year."

Archie had a keen eye for those who used his café all year round, and our order was soon taken. Carly slurped a mouthful of coffee then bit down on her triple-decker sandwich. Sausage cooking juices ran down her chin. She dabbed at them with a napkin then took an even larger bite. I grinned and cut a somewhat more delicate square from my slice of baked beans on toast. The breeze from the café door opening wafted across my back. Mid-drool on her second bite, Carly widened her eyes.

The soft voice that had invaded my previous night's dreams asked from behind me, "Megan?"

I turned my head, praying I didn't have bean juice smeared on my lips, but whatever light rejoinder I'd been intending to utter fled as I gazed. "Gethin?"

His irises seemed to liquify. "You sought my name as I did yours?"

My breath caught in my throat. I couldn't speak, and instead, nodded.

He smiled. "When you want me, call my name, and I'll come to you."

He walked away looking every bit as fit in mufti as he had done in elf-green, and my heart raced.

Carly pushed her sunglasses down to the tip of her nose and peered at me over the top of him. "Okay, a bit short but still okay on the gorgeous front. I approve of the jeans and white tee, although the leather trench coat could do with an update. Spit it out. Who is he?"

I watched him walk to the counter to wait for his takeout bag and gave myself a mental kick for the goofy expression I was sure was pasted on my face. "I met him in the store yesterday. He's an actor. Appearing in this year's panto, apparently."

She smirked. "Well, he certainly seems to be practicing his lines on you."

My cheeks heated. "It's more likely he's rehearsing them to chat up Susie. She's got her eye on him, so I heard."

Carly grinned. "Nah. It doesn't always work that way. Leggy girls don't float everyone's boat. He's a short-arse. You're a short-arse."

I huffed. "Well, thank you for that, I don't think."

She laughed—all signs of her hangover gone. "Get over it, girlie. You're pretty. He's damn cute. You're five-foot-three, he's probably five-seven. That's a good match, I'd say."

I glanced down at my over-ample chest, then my less-than-svelte thighs and vowed never to eat another kebab. *'Gethin with me compared to Susie? Yeah, in my dreams.'*

'Why would I want to be with a girl so tall I'd have to stand on a box to kiss her lips?'

I gave my over-active imagination a good telling off. *'Pack it in. That's wishful thinking, not a wish that could come true just because you'd like it to.'*

'I'd like it to.'

I tutted at myself and took some cash out of my purse. We divided the bill, left the money on the table, and pushed back our chairs.

Carly stowed her dark glasses in her pocket and kissed my cheek. "Thanks, Megan. I'll see you at home later."

I pecked her back. "Yeah. I'll cook and we can watch a movie, then we'll be right on form for the meet-up at the Frog and Frigate tomorrow."

She nodded. We went our separate ways, and the afternoon passed quickly. Alongside Sarah, I made so many sales I knew there would be enough commission in my month-end pay packet to make up for the fact I'd overspent on Christmas.

My feet were killing me as I let myself into my flat after work, so I kicked off my shoes, whipped up a couple of cheese omelettes, and Carly and I ate them sitting in front of the gas fire—log effect, totally fake—and watched *Home Alone*.

She turned off the set at the end credits, and I went to bed, but tired as I was after a long day at work, sleep evaded me. I settled into a half-awake dreamy state and let my mind drift. There were two more workdays to go until Christmas. When I returned to my flat after it, I would book a theatre ticket, front row. Gethin wouldn't be able to miss me sitting there. If he fancied me like Carly thought he did, he would come and find me, surely? I could hardly wait!

I woke in the morning, showered, and contemplated my wardrobe while I dressed in my staff uniform of tailored navy-blue trousers and pink logo'd shirt. A cherry-coloured velvet dress caught my eye. Its skirt was flared which would soothe my habitual self-consciousness over the state of my kebab-laden thighs. The waist cinched with a belt which was flattering, although it did rather emphasise the fulsome mounds above it—but then everything did. The fact I was top-heavy for my height couldn't be hidden, and I wondered what a certain elf thought of that.

'Beautiful...'

Beautiful? Where the hell had that come from? I shut the wardrobe door with a sharp snap, shouted goodbye to Carly, and left the flat. My car was parked outside, but I didn't use it for my daily commute—the parking charges in the city centre were too high, and instead I took the bus.

It was standing room only. Passengers packed in like sardines jostled each other, but good-naturedly with a smile and a passing comment on what they had left to buy, what with it being Christmas Eve tomorrow. We chugged past the college that had brought me to the city ten years previously—the small village I'd grown up in not able to boast of an educational facility past high school, and nothing had attracted me to return to live there after I graduated.

I sometimes felt guilty for not finding work that made use of my degree in fine arts, but I'd started working for Robins and Son as a Saturday job to top up my student grant, and with a recession looming, had stayed on full-time. With some help from my parents, I'd scraped up the deposit needed to purchase my flat, and the rent I received from letting the second bedroom ensured I could afford the mortgage payments.

'Santa Claus is coming to town. Santa Claus is coming to town…'

Sarah hummed along to the tune and gave me a happy smile when I joined her behind the counter. "Last day for me. Felicity can moan all she likes, but I'm owed a day in lieu and I'm not working tomorrow."

Her good humour was infectious, and I smiled. "No prizes for guessing that Dave's also got the day off, I suppose?"

She pointed to a store bag under the counter. "Take a peek inside. I snagged it from Lingerie on my way through the store this morning. The price had been reduced to tempt the last-minute punters to open their wallets."

I twitched it open and saw red satin panties with a matching peek-a-boo bra of a flimsiness that definitely didn't come in my size of triple D.

"Blimey! Dave's eyes will be popping out of his head when he sees this in the flesh, so to speak."

Sarah giggled, and Felicity gave us the evil eye, so I moved to the till and tapped the numerical code that identified my sales onto the keypad. The doors opened, and people flooded into the store. Around mid-morning, a flash of green caught my eye. I bagged my customer's purchase and handed it over. He moved away, and Gethin took his place.

My heart raced at the sight of him, but I swallowed hard and managed to keep my voice even. "Oh, hi. Are you working in the grotto today?"

He shook his head and smiled into my eyes. "I don't work with anyone other than the main man in red, and he's got a job elsewhere today. I'm just using my coffee break to check my special girl's okay."

My special girl? As in, he's already got a girlfriend? Damn! It must be Susie he's here to see.

I willed my pulse to settle and, faced with a healthy dose of reality, it did. "I won't hold you up then. Have a good day."

I turned to the next customer needing to be served, rang the Chanel No5 he'd chosen through the till, and dropped it into a small carrier bag with a bright smile. "A lovely choice, sir. Some lady is going to be delighted come Christmas morning."

My customer was rather short of festive cheer and grunted. "At the best part of a hundred quid, she'd better be."

Sarah must have overheard him and caught my eye with the coded glance all sales assistants knew and shared—*wanker!*

I kept my smile fixed to my face despite my urge to grin, then noticed Gethin hadn't moved.

"Ah…" he said. "I'd like to try some of the samples, please?"

I picked up a booklet of test strips, not feeling particularly overjoyed at the prospect of helping to choose this particular gift, but ten years of service stood me in good stead, and my expression didn't waver as I moved to his side of the counter. "Sure. What base notes does she like? Woody, floral, spicy?"

The smile that lit his eyes was wickedly mischievous. "I haven't a clue. I might have to smell them all."

If I hadn't known better, I would have suspected a ruse so he could spend time in my company, but unfortunately I did, and led the way to the rack that contained the range of Rive Gauche products that surrounded Susie in an invisible cloud whenever she walked past me. I selected those either side of it so he wouldn't know I'd guessed. He shook his head at my first two offerings, then to the third I'd been sure he'd recognise. I ploughed on, and his tuts and huffs became more and more outrageous until I laughed.

"Okay, at least give me a hint of what you're searching for."

He leaned closer, sniffed, then pointed over my shoulder. I knew which display was behind me. His nasal detective work was right on the mark. I selected the identical bottle to the one I'd squirted myself with at home earlier—Woman by Jasper Conran—and offered it to him. "This one?"

He looked so pleased with himself I supposed I should be flattered he liked my choice of perfume so much he wanted to buy it for someone else. I wasn't, though, and took it to the till, mentally consigning my own atomiser to the next charity donation bag that plonked onto my front door mat.

I giftwrapped it, and he asked while I did so, "What have you got planned for Christmas? I'm working over the holidays myself."

I handed him his purchase. "I've got a girls' night out at the Frog and Frigate after work, then I'm back here manning the counters tomorrow, and once the store closes I'll drive to my parents' house and spend Christmas with my family."

Jess muttered as she passed behind me, "Step it up, will you? We're not going to get double-bubble if you spend an hour with each customer."

My cheeks heated. At Robins and Son, the department with the highest sales figures during December had the commission they'd earned paid twice over. I handed Gethin his gift receipt, turned away, and mouthed my apology at her. "Sorry. I'm on it now."

In the next hour, I moved like lightning, and between them, half a dozen customers spent the best part of a grand. Felicity printed out each of our running tabs after lunch—a break I hadn't taken.

Jess peered over my shoulder. "Damn! How did you manage that?

With thoughts of a three-course meal after the store closed, I shrugged nonchalantly. "I worked through."

She poked me in the ribs. "Teacher's pet."

I poked her back. "You won't be complaining come the end of the month."

Two mince pies plugged the hole at afternoon break. Sarah and Dave chatted only with each other. Ronnie and I ran out of conversation and sipped the last of our tea in silence. I headed back to the shop floor before break was officially over and managed to ring another two thousand pounds through the till by the time the concierge ushered the last customer through the double-width glass doors. I requested the total daily sales tally from it and offered Sarah a high-five. She smacked my hand, and Amber and Jess rushed over.

Jess looked at the close-of-business figure displayed in bright red LED and grinned. "We smashed it today."

Felicity gave us a rare smile. "You certainly did. Keep it up. You all know what's at stake."

The air felt distinctly chillier than it had in the morning as I waited at the bus stop. I shivered, pulled my padded jacket tighter around my body, and decided my heavier, full-length coat would be coming out of the wardrobe to wear over my dress when I returned to the town centre later.

Carly was home and had turned the heating up. My hands and feet slowly defrosted while I made a welcome cup of tea. I relaxed on the sofa to drink it, and she buzzed around the flat gathering items to pack for her morning departure to her boyfriend Mark's family home to spend Christmas with his parents.

Her muffled voice floated through the doorway from the depths of the shoe cupboard in the hall. "Have you seen my fur-lined boots? We're in for a right bout of sleety crap over the next day or two, the weather forecast said."

I moved to help her look.

"Don't worry. Got 'em. Right at the back. Do you want yours?"

"Yeah. I better had." With no meal to cook, I'd been planning a long soak in the bathtub but decided to pack the car in advance rather than wait until after I got home after work on Christmas Eve if the weather was due to deteriorate. I would fork out the overnight car park charges, drive myself and Carly into town, and leave the car overnight. If I took a bus or taxi ride home, my car would be on hand when the store closed.

I started by stacking my wrapped gifts by the front door then tugged my travel holdall from the top of the wardrobe. It didn't take long to fill. I already knew which clothes I needed to take with me—thick sweaters and jeans, underwear, and a pretty dress to wear on Christmas Day. Next, I shrugged on a thick anorak along with my boots and opened the front door. A freezing gust nearly slammed it closed in my face. The wind had certainly gathered force in the hour.

Carly hurried forward and leaned her weight against it to keep it open for me. "Where'd that come from already?"

An icy blast carried my reply away. "Bloody hell!"

My car, an elderly but reliable Toyota, started up first time, and I left the engine running so I could switch on its lights and see what I was doing. Three trips back and forth filled the boot, then I turned everything off and staggered back inside with relief.

I walked to the kitchen and hung my anorak on the back of a chair. Carly made us both a steaming black coffee and splashed a tot of brandy into each.

She clunked her mug against mine. "Cheers. That's us all good to go. Have you decided what you're wearing tonight?"

I took a large gulp and coughed when the strong spirit hit the back of my throat. She laughed and thumped my back.

I recovered my breath and answered, "My cherry velvet dress with the skater skirt."

She nodded knowingly at my upper legs. "We've all got a bit of ourselves we'd like to change, but I've never heard anyone say your thighs are too chunky."

I swallowed a smaller sip. "It's a childhood thing, I think. In story books and films, short and female equates to petite, cute, pixie types, and I'm not that."

"No. You're curvy but in all the right places as I'd say the guy in Archie's café very much appreciated."

My heart leapt, and I couldn't keep the grin off my face. "You think?"

She laughed. "I know so, so what are you going to do about it?"

"I thought about booking a ticket and going to watch the pantomime after Christmas if Gethin's in it. Sort of near the front so he'd see me."

She picked up her phone. "What are they putting on this year? Have you checked the cast list?"

"Ah...no."

She tapped then gave it to me. "There you go. It's not a traditional panto this year. The Festival Theatre is offering a Christmas Spectacular of show tunes, apparently."

I took it and read...

Come and enjoy a musical feast for the whole family. Songs for all ages, young and old, presented with a large helping of Festive Cheer. Featuring...

Let It Go – Think of Me – White Christmas – A Kiss To Build A Dream On – Jingle Bells – Santa Claus Is Coming To Town…and many more!

Included in the ticket price: A present for every child from Santa's sack! A glass of mulled wine for the over 18s!

That explained the need for a Mr Claus and his helper, but something else about the playbill thrilled me. I couldn't quite put my finger on what it was—but an evening of song and dance was much more up my street than *Snow White and the Seven Dwarfs* or *Aladdin* with the prospect of Widow Twanky. I set my mug on the table as I noted my phone displaying the time—six-forty-five. "We'd best move it and get our glad rags on if we're meeting the girls at eight. I'm leaving the car in town overnight, so I'll drive us there and we can share a cab home."

Several of the girls were seated at a table when we arrived at the restaurant—although *girls* was quite a loose term for a disparate group that included a couple of Carly's friends in their early twenties along with our next-door neighbours, June and Barb, in their fifties and sixties respectively, who we socialised with at quiz nights held at the local pub. They were all getting on like a house on fire, though. Christmas party nights at the Frog and Frigate were legendary.

Tables had been pushed together to form an open E around three sides of the room, leaving the central floor space free for when the dance music revved up. Each was dressed with brightly coloured themed paperware—table coverings, serviettes, Christmas crackers, baskets of streamers, and party poppers. Wine was included in the cover price, along with the three-course meal. Silverware sparkled, glasses were full, and the volume of happy chatter was already loud.

Carly grinned. "This is more like it. My office do was pretty good, but there was no dancing or crackers, and it's not a proper Christmas party unless you're wearing a silly paper crown."

I agreed. "That and reading out the same jokes and riddles that you did last year."

She laughed. "What's yellow and dangerous?"

I called out the answer to the pun my grandmother swore had been in the first Christmas cracker she'd pulled when they became available again after World War Two. "Shark-infested custard."

"Oh God, not that old chestnut," June hooted as we sat at the table. There was large jug of what looked like margarita standing in between her and Barb.

Carly's friend, Beth, giggled. "They've been getting a head start on the rest of us."

"The cocktail list is on the table if you want to order one," June said.

I picked it up, and knowing I had to be up for work in the morning, ordered the least lethal mix I could see from the hovering waiter. "I'll take a strawberry daiquiri, thanks."

Carly peered over my arm. "A Cosmo, please."

"Make it a jug," Carly's other friend, Kirsty, added.

Crackers were pulled to a chorus of laughs and groans when the ancient shark motto, now funny for never having been funny, made its usual appearance. Paper hats were donned, and the food arrived. It wasn't fabulous, dinner being a facilitator to the imbibing of alcohol, not the highlight of the evening.

Our group managed to empty four bottles of wine by the time the remnants of the meal were cleared. Beth and Kirsty, with the hollow legs of those under twenty-five, ordered another jug of cocktail to share. The DJ increased the volume of the music, and I soaked up the party atmosphere.

Christmas pop mingled with party classics. I loved it.

The dance floor filled. I hoisted Beth to her feet after we'd indulged in an enthusiastic rendition of *Oops Upside Your Head*. Gloria Estefan's voice poured out of the speakers, and a conga line began to form. Beth joined the end of it with Kirsty behind her, but before I could position myself behind them, a hand touched my arm. I swung around and came face to face with Gethin. He took a sprig of mistletoe from his pocket.

Beth giggled when the line moved off. "Ooh, you're cute. Back in a min. Save me a snog spot."

He ignored her and smiled into my eyes. "I came prepared. Can I have my kiss?"

My innards did a squidgy melty thing, and I gazed back. "Oh…"

He stepped closer. My heart raced. My knees trembled. He put his arms around me and his lips on mine. I tasted his mouth, and my body responded, but as he deepened our kiss, the frenzied snaking dance whirled past. Beth exited the line.

Kirsty tugged me into it and laughed. "Don't be so greedy, Megan. Let someone else have a go."

I was swept away, and Gethin shouted to me, "Call me."

"I haven't got your mobile number."

"You don't need it. Just call me…"

I lost sight of him. The music changed to *The Birdie Song*. The conga line split apart, and the party crowd filled the center of the room, but there was no sign of Gethin.

Beth joined me and pouted. "Well, he wasn't much fun, was he? I closed my eyes and puckered up, but he legged it."

Carly appeared and looked at Beth, her face furious. "How could you? I told you yesterday my flatmate had met a bloke she really liked. Shoulder-length brown hair tied back. Tom Cruise size, but cuter. Remember?"

Beth giggled tipsily. "Oopsie. Sorry."

I squeezed Carly's hand, the mistletoe in Gethin's hand and a song title from the theatre's advertised playlist tugging at my memory. "It's okay. If he likes me enough, he'll turn up at the store again." I headed towards our table.

Carly accompanied me. "Sorry, babe. I'll have a few words with her when she sobers up. That was out of order."

I reached for the purse I'd stowed out of sight under my chair when I'd got up to dance and took my phone out of it. "No worries. Don't let it spoil your evening."

"So long as it hasn't ruined yours?"

I shook my head, tapped Google, and entered the words Gethin had said to me the first time we met in the staff canteen. The words of a song appeared on the screen. *'Give me a kiss to build a dream on. Sweetheart, I ask no more than this…'*

I gazed. Was it me he wanted to be 'his special girl', not Susie? I knew my hopeful delight must be plastered all over my face when Carly grinned.

"What is it? You've found something, haven't you?" she asked.

I turned my phone around. "The opening line is what Gethin said to me when we were on afternoon break at work the other day. The song is one of the numbers listed on the theatre playbill."

She read the screen, laughed, and offered me a high-five. "I knew it! The way he looked at you in Archie's was a dead giveaway."

I smacked her hand with mine, and she downed the last of her drink.

"Shall we call it quits, babe?" she said. "We've had a fab time, but Mark's not here, and Beth's scared off your man."

I nodded. We phoned for a taxi and said our goodbyes. The wind had calmed from what it was earlier, but icy bullets still pelted us as we ran from the venue and jumped into the warm interior of the hackney cab.

Carly shut our front door behind us and puffed out. "Jeez, it's nothing like a Christmas card out there. Soft fluffy snow, bah humbug! I hope this shite clears up by tomorrow."

Her hopes were not realised.

I woke in the morning and hugged the happy thought to myself. *It's Christmas Eve.* However, the weather had taken a turn for the worse again. Sleety gusts of rain thundered against the windowpane, and I was glad I'd prepacked the car and could get a head start on the drive to my mum and dad's after work. Carly sat at the kitchen table eating a piece of hot buttered toast when I walked into the room.

She waved at the bread bin. "I saved you a couple of slices, and there's still enough milk in the fridge for a coffee."

I nodded. "What time are you setting off?"

"Straight after breakfast. Mark's picking me up at nine. It'll be a slow trip with the windscreen wipers going at double speed, but we should arrive at his parents' house before ten, even with a service stop at Leigh Delaware."

I yawned then picked up my coffee mug. "I've only got a two-hour drive. Even with being at work until five, I'll probably be home before you cross the border into Scotland."

She agreed, and in high expectation of receiving double-bubble at the end of the month, I blew my budget and phoned for a taxi to take me to work.

I half hoped Gethin might turn up, but as lunch time approached, it occurred to me that even if the freezing downpour hadn't been enough of a put-off, he was probably in last-minute rehearsals if he was part of the Festival Theatre's show which opened in a couple of hours with a matinee performance.

The canteen was lively. On Christmas Eve, Robins and Son always laid on a complimentary buffet for staff working right up until the store closed. Staff relaxed and enjoyed the food, happy in the knowledge that as we didn't open for business on Christmas Day, and having just worked a full shift, none of us would be required to man the counters until at least the twenty-seventh. I filled a plate with pasta salad and sausage rolls to keep me going until I could tuck into the rich, savoury stew my mother would have waiting for me, then sat and gossiped with Carol from Homewares until my hour was up.

Customers were a little thin on the ground during the afternoon, and there was no last-minute rush to delay us running to the locker room to grab our coats, shout Merry Christmas, and leave by the back door.

I turned the collar of my coat up against freezing lumps of hail the wind was attempting to shove down my neck. My car was a welcome sight, now sitting in near isolation in the middle of the car park. I unlocked the doors, jumped in, set the hot air switch to high, and turned the key in the ignition. There was a dull clunk. I tried again. *Clunk.* And again. *Clunk.*

I muttered, "Bugger it!" With the radio, heater, and headlights on last night, the drive into town couldn't have been far enough for the alternator to replace the power I'd used, and the battery was flat.

I swore again, reached for the breakdown recovery certificate I kept in the glove box, and gave them a call. The lady who answered assured me help was on the way, although with an apology for their being dreadfully busy, the icy conditions having led to a high volume of callouts.

I wasn't unduly concerned. When the mechanic arrived, I only needed a jump-start which at most would take a matter of minutes. I settled back into my seat, texted my mum to tell her I would be home a little a later than expected, and whiled away the first hour scrolling through Facebook. During the second hour, I shivered, despite the padded thickness of my winter coat. My plaid picnic blanket was folded on the back seat, so I reached for it and wrapped it around myself. I longed for a hot drink to warm me but didn't dare leave the car to go in search of one in case the rescue vehicle turned up when I was gone.

I fretted when the time ticked over into the third hour, but as I contemplated phoning the breakdown company again, headlights illuminated the car park. I opened the door, waved, and the truck pulled up alongside. A uniformed driver got out of it, his high-vis jacket bearing the legend: *Greg. Roadside Rescue Service*. "Cor, bleeding brass monkeys out here innit, love? Flat battery, they said. Pop the bonnet for me."

I tugged on the lever. He attached leads from a super charger on an upright wheeled trolley to my battery. "Turn her over, darlin…"

I twisted the key. *Clunk.* Then again. The engine coughed. And again. The car revved.

Greg opened the passenger door and climbed in. "You should be fine now, but I'll sit here for a few minutes to check your battery is charging okay."

I smiled. "Thanks. I was about to drive home to my parents' house when it wouldn't fire up."

He nodded. "It happens a lot this time of year. Windshield de-misters back and front, full-beam lights, seat and steering wheel heaters, all on, night and day. The drain on the vehicle's start-up capacity is terrific."

We sat in comfortable silence for a while until an acrid stench wafted through the heating vents. The oil light came on. The temperature gauge rose.

Greg sat straighter. "Bloody hell! Cut the ignition. Quick!"

I did so.

He jumped out and fiddled with the engine. His face did not look happy when he returned. "How long has this car been sitting here? More than just today?"

I nodded. "Yeah...since about seven-thirty last night."

He shook his head. "Thought so. Sorry, love, it's your sump. The oil's settled, and the sub-zero conditions have turned it to a thick sludge. Your engine can't heat it quickly enough to get it moving and do its job. Without lubrication, the engine will seize, and the vehicle will be a write-off."

"What? It can't be fixed?"

"Oh, it can be repaired, but it'll need a complete oil change, and that's a garage job. How far's your place? Best I can offer you is a tow within a five-mile radius."

I stared at him in stunned disbelief but didn't waste any more time exploring the issue. If my only option was to return to my flat, I needed to do so without delay so I could search for an alternative means of transport. I told him my address. He hooked my car up to his truck, and with its orange light revolving its warning, towed me home. I thanked him and rushed inside, switched on the lights, and cranked the heating up.

My first port of call was to discover whether a train was a possibility. I Googled the timetable, checked the time on my phone, and my heart sank as I realised that a Sunday service had been initiated at seven o'clock. The last train to the station nearest the village where my parents lived had already departed. Car rental was next, but unless it was already pre-booked, their offices were closed. The online quote for a long-distance taxi came back as eye-wateringly expensive as the trip would be charged at triple time. It dawned on me I would be going precisely nowhere in the next few hours, so I did what I always did in times of crisis and phoned my mum.

I told her what had happened and heard the distress in her voice. "Oh no, love. I never expected this. Fred. Fred. How much sherry have you had?"

"Three glasses. Why? What's up?"

"Damn. So have I. Megan's car has broken down."

Dad came on the phone. "I won't have another drop, Meg. As soon as I'm okay to drive I'll set off and come get you."

I pictured the scene. My nephews would be in bed, their stockings hung by the living room fire. The adults would be sitting around the kitchen table, chatting and having a glass or two while Mum stuffed the turkey and Granny peeled the sprouts. I squared my shoulders. *For goodness sake, you're nearly thirty. Grow up and take one for the team.*

"No, Dad. There's no need for you to turn out in this weather when the trains are running a Sunday timetable tomorrow. I'll get the earliest one and be with you before Mum puts lunch on the table at one."

"Oh, love, are you sure? It wouldn't be any trouble."

I tutted. "I'm a big girl now. Of course, I am."

Mum came back on the line. "I don't like the thought you waking up on Christmas morning all alone."

Neither did I, but my decision was made. "It'll be fine. I'll be with you before you know it tomorrow."

"Well…goodnight then…and don't you dare miss that train."

"I won't. Night, Mum." I felt proud of myself as I cut the call, but my bravado deserted me at the sound of nothing but silence in my flat. I thought perhaps the hot drink I'd been longing for might help, and while the kettle boiled, exchanged my work clothes for a pair of soft pyjamas.

The fridge was suitably empty with both Carly and I expecting to be away for several days, although there were a couple of eggs in it that didn't go out of date until the following week. I found I didn't have much of an appetite for them when I should have been tucking into Mum's home-cooked stew, so I shut the fridge door and took a mug of hot lemon tea into the sitting room.

The tree lights, television, and gas fire switched on, I sat on the sofa and flicked through the channels which proved to be a mistake. Each programme I paused on was seemingly a seasonal special featuring loved-up couples and excited children which only brought home to me—it was Christmas Eve, and I was Billy-no-mates. I pressed the remote, the screen went blank, and I finished my drink, contemplating the flames flickering over the artificial logs of the gas fire.

A pang of loneliness settled in the pit of my stomach. Here I was again, the unwilling singleton, when everyone else was in couples or pairs. That wasn't true, I knew, but it was how I felt at times—like I was the odd one out, the third wheel, the spare guest at the feast invited along to make up the numbers. I closed my eyes and relived my mistletoe kiss, longing for another. "I wish you were here with me, Gethin."

'Of course, cariad. You only had to call me.'

His voice seemed more substantial than an echo of memory. I opened my eyes. Small sparkles like glittering motes of dust danced in front of them, settled, then solidified. I blinked, debating whether the lemon juice I'd used in my tea could have been 'off' in a manner that made it in anyway alcoholic, although the hallucination, if that's what it was, looked solidly three-dimensional and mouth-wateringly gorgeous. I wondered if in my rush to get indoors I hadn't properly latched the front door and found I didn't care how he'd got into my flat, only that he had.

"Gethin? You're here?"

He gazed into my eyes. "You're happy that I am?"

I nodded. The emerald of his irises darkened a shade or several, and he pulled his sprig of mistletoe from his pocket. "I believe I only got half my kiss last night?"

My heart soared. "I think I did, too."

He sat beside me on the sofa, and I moved into his arms. His lips were soft on mine as I tilted my face to his. I opened my mouth for his tongue and tasted his, my breasts pressed on his hard chest. He cupped the back of my head, kissed me harder, and my body responded, my nipples hardening, aching for his touch.

He moved his mouth and kissed under my ear. "So, Megan Jones, are we going to be naughty or nice?"

I took his hand, urged it up inside my top, and placed it on my braless breast then brushed my fingers across the bulge of his stiffening crotch. "Oh, we're going to be very naughty indeed."

His breath hissed between his teeth. "Yes, cariad…please."

I looked into his eyes, saw a hunger to match mine, and reached for the zip on his jeans. His cock pushed against the confines of the material, and I couldn't move the zipper past it, so I tugged his top out of the waistband. He pulled it off over his head, and my breath caught when his smooth chest and the defined muscles of his belly appeared. I unbuttoned my pyjama top, shrugged it off over my shoulders, and the intensity of his gaze told me he liked what he saw very much.

He toed off his half-boots, stood, unfastened his jeans, and freed his swollen cock. My heart rate increased, my pussy throbbing with desire to feel him inside me. I inched my PJ bottoms downwards and off. Naked, he stepped closer. I lay back on the sofa and welcomed him into my arms. His warm skin on mine felt so good, I wanted to touch all of him at once.

He kissed my lips then the soft skin under my ear. "You're beautiful, cariad. I've dreamed of this since we met."

I smiled and tilted my head for more. "So, every time you've seen me you've been picturing me naked?"

He moved his mouth downwards to my shoulder. "And you haven't me?"

That was the truth, although the reality was even fitter than my imagination could provide. I ran my hands over his shoulders and explored the contours of his back. "Yeah, I have."

He cupped my breast and covered my nipple with his mouth. My pussy dampened as he kneaded and sucked, his hard cock pressing on my thigh. I longed for a taste, but the high-backed sofa didn't have the wriggle room of a double bed. I parted my legs and wrapped them around him so I could reach down and touch. He murmured with pleasure when I grasped his shaft and turned his attention to my other breast. His cock felt so good, smooth and thick. I moved my hand up down its length and he nipped my nipple with his teeth.

My pussy throbbed, and I breathed, "Oh…yes…"

I wanted him inside me. He did it again a little harder. I grasped his butt checks and urged him higher.

He lifted his head. "Now…?"

"God, yes."

He stroked through the folds of my pussy and slipped one finger then another inside me. I ground down against them. They weren't enough. I needed his cock. "Please, now."

He raised his hips and replaced his fingers with the tip of his shaft. I increased the grip of my legs around him. His shaft moved deeper.

"Yes, cariad. Squeeze your thighs around me. Hold me tight."

I did so and sighed as he thrust, slowly at first then harder and faster when I dug my fingertips into his back. Panting, I tilted my pelvis to meet his. The pressure built on my sweet spot with every stroke until muscles tightened at the center of my pussy and I bucked beneath him, the shockwaves of my climax spreading.

"Yes, Gethin. Yes…"

He grasped my breasts, one in each hand, and rode me faster, then groaned low in his throat. "Beautiful. So beautiful."

We stilled, breathing hard. Gethin withdrew and rested his cheek on my breast, his eyes closed, his expression contentedly blissful. I smiled. A lover who delighted in their partner's plumpness hopefully wouldn't be turned off by the utilitarian nature of the corsetry I was obliged to wear to support them when dressed.

He nestled closer. "Course not. It's just window dressing."

I experienced a brief moment of déjà vu as he replied to a thought I hadn't said out loud. This had happened before, in the canteen the first time we'd met, at Archie's café—and even more surreal, if the words that occasionally popped into my head out of nowhere lately were his not mine, he didn't have to be anywhere near me to do so. "Ah… Gethin… Can you sort of hear what I'm thinking or something?"

He smiled. "Not always, cariad. Only if we're thinking of each other at the same time. Then your words reach me, and mine you."

I strived to rationalise his answer. "So, like a mind-reading act? Did they teach you the trick of how to do it at stage school?"

He sat a little straighter, loosened the leather thong at the nape of his neck, and tucked his hair behind his ear. It was more than definitely pointed, although not of the flamboyant proportions portrayed in works of fiction. "The main man in red likes to get out and about a bit in the run-up the big day, so we take a temporary job here and there. I'm no more an actor than he is. We are true-born elves, cariad."

He gazed into my eyes. I stroked my fingertips down his face. It was solid, warm, and real, so why did I get the feeling Gethin would dissolve before my eyes as suddenly as he had appeared if what I said next wasn't what he needed to hear?

'You know why, cariad.'

His words floated into my mind, and as they did, it clicked. The fundamental principle on which the legend rested. Santa Claus and his elves only existed for those who believed. Did I?

Could I? Our lovemaking had been no illusion. I'd felt a connection between us since our eyes first met. My heart melted at the anxiousness I saw enter his at my hesitation, and the answer to the questions I'd asked myself became easy. Yes, and yes.

"So, you are. What is a cariad?"

He laid his cheek back on my breast with a soft sigh. "All rolled into one word…my sweetheart, my darling, my love. I knew it from the start. I could hear your thoughts so clearly and you mine. We are heart-bound, cariad."

I adored the sound of that and stroked the back of his head. "I feel it, too. I've had boyfriends in the past but never felt this way about anyone before. Will we be able to see each other during the rest of the year?"

"Sure. December is pretty hectic work-wise, but I get a fair bit of downtime from the day job the rest of the year."

There was no way I wasn't going to ask. "Day job?"

He smiled as if expecting the question, reached for his jeans, and took a tiny silver box out of the pocket. "Guarding the deep mine from those who would plunder its contents if they knew what it contained."

Intrigued, I sat straighter. "And that is?"

He eased off the tightly fitted lid. Inside was a small amount of the sparkling motes I'd seen earlier. "Magic."

My mind boggled as I peered at it. "It that fairy dust? Like you see in children's books and films?"

He replaced the lid, put it back into his pocket, and slipped on his jeans. "That's one name for it, although in actuality, it's stardust. The original magic that kick-started the universe into being. The only place it can be found on Earth is in the strata below our Elven caverns. It's how we get the whole Christmas gig done, and given its power, why we hide its existence."

I scooped up my pyjamas and thought of the possibilities while I put them on. "Wow. Yeah. I can think of several world leaders I wouldn't like to see anywhere near it, and it doesn't take much imagination to know what psychopaths like Hitler would have done with it."

Gethin nodded and pulled on his tee. "Our caverns lie beneath two miles of solid ice at the polar cap. They're nearly impossible to reach except by using dust, but we keep a wary eye on a number of current drilling explorations searching for oil and gas."

"Can't you just use your magic dust to make them disappear?"

234

He laughed. "Well, we could, but it might give the game away if people and equipment started turning up unexpectedly in a shower of sparkles. We do employ a little stardust, though. Their test data never displays a positive result within a five-mile radius of our caverns, but the majority of the dust we take from the mine is used as it always has been for nearly two thousand years. To continue the Christmas legacy started by our founding father, St Nic."

"Wow! Santa is that old? He doesn't look it."

Gethin smiled. "No, cariad. He's not. The Elven race is no more immortal than anybody else. St Nic was the first, but he's had many personas since. Kris Kringle, Father Christmas, and Santa Claus—they've all been the elf of elves, the wisest of us all."

A thought occurred to me. "Ah…it's Christmas Eve. Shouldn't you be working?"

"No. Santa works this part alone. Most children don't go short of a gift at Christmas nowadays, so of the those who write in, the nice list is comprised of the believers who wouldn't receive a present, if not from him."

I smiled. "I was wondering how that worked, being as most children's stockings are filled by their parents. I thought you and Santa were working a Christmas stint at the Festival Theatre at first, you know?"

He winked. "Well, we did audition but didn't get the part. The song list we were given came in handy, though."

I couldn't keep the grin from my face. "Well, for that, I ought to offer you a coffee, I suppose."

He jumped to his feet and tugged me upright. "Yes, you should. Show me your home? I've been trying to picture it."

I led the way to the kitchen. Gethin peered interestedly about him, and I gave him the rundown. "My bedroom is the door on the right. The second bedroom beside it, I rent out to Carly— that's the girl you saw me with in Archie's café. She's spending Christmas with her boyfriend's family. Opposite is the bathroom, and straight ahead is the kitchen, and that's the lot, apart from a small patch of garden out the back."

We arrived at my neat and compact kitchen, and Gethin asked, "Why are you not at your parents' house where you said you'd be?"

I filled the kettle and flicked the switch for it to boil. "My car wouldn't start, so the breakdown service towed me home. I'll catch a train in the morning. They're running a slow service, but I'll get there. Sorry, I'm out of milk. Black coffee or lemon tea?"

"Lemon sounds good, and don't worry about your car. It'll start just fine in the morning. I promise."

I handed him his drink. "Courtesy of your little silver box?"

He sipped and nodded.

I leaned closer and kissed his cheek. "Thank you. I really wasn't overly thrilled at the thought of lugging all my gear onto a draughty train."

Gethin smiled and set down his mug. "I should go. We form a guard of honour to welcome Santa back home. I mustn't miss it. Perhaps next year you'd like to be there, too? We could visit your family after."

The prospect was everything I'd dreamed of. "Absolutely, I would. I can't wait!"

He looked as happy as I felt and put his arms around me. "Let's promise not spend Christmas apart again, cariad."

I lifted my face for his kiss. "I promise."

His kiss was deep and lingering, then he took the magic dust out of his pocket. "Call me when you're back here?"

I smiled and nodded. Gethin flicked open the lid and with a pinch of sparkles was gone.

I walked to my bedroom feeling as if I was walking on air, slipped under the duvet, and with a contented sigh, closed my eyes.

I stirred in the morning, grey fingers of light curling around the edges of the curtains, so switched on the lamp standing on top of my bedside cabinet. A Robins and Son giftbag was on it. It seemed very much like the one I'd handed to Gethin in the store, and I grinned with delight when I opened it and found a sprig of mistletoe sitting on top the bottle of Jasper Conran perfume I'd thought was destined for Susie. *'I adore it, Gethin.'*

'Happy Christmas, cariad. Drive safe.'

Excited shivers tingled down my spine. It was Christmas morning, and I was not alone. I was half of a couple now. *'I will, and Happy Christmas to you, darling.'*

There was sound of wind and rain as I swung my legs out of bed and walked to the bathroom to take a shower. The water was hot, and I sang *Jingle Bells* at the top of my voice while I soaped up. My hair I rough-dried then dressed in jeans and sweater—my Christmas dress I would change into when I arrived at my parents'. My phone was vibrating on the coffee table when I went into the sitting room. I picked it up and saw a missed call and three text messages from my mum.

Happy Christmas. Are you up?

Why aren't you answering? I hope you're not still asleep.

MEGAN!

I checked the time. It wasn't yet eight o'clock. I messaged her back.

Sorry. Was in shower. Happy Christmas. Car fixed. Be home before eleven.

I gulped down a black coffee and half an hour later jumped into my Toyota. It fired straight up as Gethin had promised it would, so I backed out of the drive and got on my way. I passed the time while I drove considering how much or little I should confide in my parents about my new boyfriend, and it didn't take me too long to decide they'd think I'd lost the plot if I informed them I was going out with a real-life elf. I decided I would tell them about Gethin, but not *all* about Gethin. I had presumed he was an actor and would leave them with that impression as well.

I parked on my parents' driveway shortly after eleven and peeped the horn. The front door opened as I heaved my travel holdall from the boot. My nephews, Alex and Sam, rushed through it, their voices piping with excitement.

"Auntie Megan. Come and see what Santa has brought us."

"We've only opened our stockings. We waited to have our presents from under the tree till you got here."

I smiled and held my arms out. "Happy Christmas, boys. Where are my big hugs?"

They scooted closer. I gave them both a hard squeeze and gestured towards the boot. "Put my gifts with the rest then. Don't drop them. They might break."

They moved like lightning but carried them inside with care. I locked the car, followed them in, and the smell of Christmas enveloped me like a warm blanket—pine, spiced fruit, and roasting meat. Heavenly.

Mum bustled out of the kitchen. "Happy Christmas, love. You made good time."

Dad followed her out. "How come your car suddenly started?"

My cheeks flushed at first mentioning him. "It wasn't sudden. Ah… I've got a new boyfriend, Gethin. He fixed it."

"Is he nice, love?" Mum asked a little anxiously.

"I like him…rather a lot actually."

Dad smiled. "That's good enough for me. Break open the bubbly, folks. Sam and Alex will explode if they have to wait much longer for their presents."

I quickly changed into my dress, and Granny and Grandpa added their Happy Christmases when I walked into the sitting room with my glass.

I sat next to Rob, my brother, and chinked my glass on his. "Merry Christmas. Let's hope it's a good one."

He looked at the towering pile of gifts wrapped in brightly coloured paper. "It will be."

Sam and Alex were ecstatic with their haul, and the Nintendo was set up. Mum called us to sit to lunch promptly at one, and I waddled away from the table afterwards stuffed so full of turkey and Christmas pudding I could barely breathe.

Later in the afternoon when I woke from my armchair snooze, I took on allcomers at Mario and thrashed them—my previous skill on the more antiquated system of my teens still holding good—with the exception of my nephews. I gave them a good battle then allowed my hand to accidentally slip so they won. My brother said losing was character-building and showed them no such leniency.

The boys went to bed around eight-thirty, and Dad broke open the bar. I asked Dad for a rum and coke, then Grandpa set up the card table, and we played silly games like Chase-The-Ace, Old Maid, and Go Fish until midnight, then I climbed the stairs to my childhood bedroom. Sam and Alex were sound asleep on an air mattress on the floor, and I tiptoed quietly to my narrow single bed so as not to wake them.

It was as saggy as I remembered it when I climbed under the duvet. The springs creaked beneath my weight as I lay down, like they always did. It was comforting and familiar, and I fell asleep in an instant.

The following morning, the boys woke me at eight and, as ever, our Boxing Day was more of the same but without the frenetic present opening. The gifts we'd received were examined more thoroughly, with instruction booklets being read and batteries inserted where necessary. Lunch was cold cuts with pickles and fries, and when relaxing in front of the television during the afternoon, I wondered what Gethin was up to. To my delight, his reply was immediate.

'Counting the hours until I see you, cariad.'

I smiled. *'And me you. Only one more day.'*

The twenty-seventh dawned with a thick frost and a clear-blue sky which boded well for a fast drive back to the city. My excitement built the closer I got. Carly wasn't due to return until the New Year, and I wasn't working until the following day. I had a whole afternoon, evening, and night I could spend with Gethin.

I dropped my holdall inside the front door after I parked, turned up the thermostat, and raced to the shower, then, smelling fresh with my hair blow-dried, poked through my underwear drawer for the only garment I possessed that was remotely sexy. It was stuffed at the very back—a belted satin robe I'd bought in the expectation of the weather being hot when I went on vacation. It hadn't been. The sky had remained stubbornly overcast for the whole two weeks.

Gethin's gift to me was beside my bed, and I treated myself to a generous spray of it. The sitting room felt chilly and dank when I entered it, so I ignited the gas fire on and lit the tree. They made a welcoming difference. My heart raced, and my skin tingled with anticipation. I gazed at the fireplace and called, "Gethin. I'm home."

Sparkles of light danced before my eyes, then settled, and my innards did a dance of joy as Gethin smiled into my eyes. "See, this elf's not just for Christmas."

I pictured Carly's face if my new boyfriend kept entering and exiting the flat by way of the fire and giggled. I danced into his arms. "I think I'd best get you a key cut for the front door then..."

Elle's Christmas Surprise

Raven McAllan

Chapter One

E lvis sang *It'll be lonely this Christmas*. Elle groaned and flicked the music off.

That was all she needed. She was not going to be lonely this Christmas, because as far as she was concerned, Christmas was a no-no event. No silly songs, no stupid parties disguised as a dance, gathering or a gala, and no pretend jollity. *Definitely no dances.* She was spending the two days she wasn't working with a good bottle of wine, a good book, and a good steak.

And a good bloke? Ha, not even in my dreams. No way. Been there, not revisiting it.

Elle might have guessed Deb would argue the toss.

"What do you mean you're not going? You have to go." Deb, all five foot two of her, glared at her twin and crossed her eyes. She reminded Elle of a picture of a ferocious elf they had both loved as kids—albeit with long, streaky blue hair.

Elle loved her fourteen-minutes-younger sister but could have enough of her company and caustic comments at times. As in that moment.

"No, I don't. You tell me where it says, Elle Harper *must* attend." Elle waved the somewhat creased invitation—due to Elle having thrown it onto the table several days before Deb saw it, grabbed it, and checked it out—in front of her twin. "Nowhere, that's where. It's just a generic invitation gone to goodness knows how many people. They won't miss me."

And there's no way I'm going to go and pretend to be happy and all gaga over Christmas. Never, ever, not even if the alternative is to be nibbled to death by ducks. Not a Scooby's chance.

If only she'd thought about it and hidden the darned thing, or binned it when it arrived, but she

248

hadn't. Then when she and Deb had been having a quick, and sneaky, coffee while there were no customers in Cosy Crafts, Elle's small, but in her eyes perfect, craft shop sandwiched between Deb's Delights—her twin's café—and Oscar Prenderville's Barber's, she could have denied all knowledge of it. Instead, Deb had noticed it and pounced on it.

"Have you replied?" Deb said as she waved it in the air. "We can go dress hunting."

"No, and not going to. Go or answer."

"I'll miss you," Deb wailed. "I can't go alone."

Elle narrowed her eyes. "You didn't say you had an invite."

Deb did her best to appear insouciant, and in Elle's eyes, failed by a country mile.

"I didn't have the opportunity, it came the other day. We were crazy busy, and you were away on your buying trip. It seems all of us in Chandler's Row have one. Which, my dear sis, should have been RSVP'd to by today. The consortium that owns the row wants to reward us for all our hard work in making the area a success. And Lord Wrenadene offered the ballroom at Chescombe Manor. It's supposed to be amazing and, well, if Oscar's going, he might for once notice me."

"Sorry, got to wash my hair that night." However, she did think Deb should go and try to catch Oscar's attention. Oscar, as far as Elle was concerned, was perfect for Deb, if only he could see it. And if Deb didn't always have a caustic comeback to his admittedly pitiful jokes.

"But...Oscar..." Deb stuttered. 'I can't go without you to chum me."

That was half the problem. Deb leaned on Elle, and Elle knew she let her. Perhaps too much. Maybe sometimes she should take a step back.

"With regards to Oscar, before you go on at me, take it from one who knows. He notices you all right, you just knock him back whenever he opens his mouth," Elle said for the umpteenth time. "You make him nervous, he says something stupid, and you pounce on it. Try smiling, or just ignoring stuff. Poor bloke probably thinks you hate him."

"Well, I don't but, honestly...anyway, stop changing the subject," Deb said. "You have to go."

"Do not."

"Do so."

What did they sound like?

"Who put you up to this?" Elle asked with mounting suspicion.

"No one," Deb said, not very convincingly. "You'll look awfully standoffish if you don't go."

"How come?" Elle swallowed the rest of her coffee and scowled through the open doorway at the Christmas display on the long table down the middle of the shop. It was only the end of November, for goodness sake. Miles too early in her mind, but it seemed not in trade. Some of the shop owners in Chandler's Row had begun decorating in early September. Until a month ago she had her seasonal table dressed for Halloween and now had it in a sort of autumn-cum-winter scenario. "It's only a bun fight, I bet lots of people won't go."

"You'll appear as if you don't want to socialise with the rest of the Row and you're up yourself. Everyone else has replied and said they're delighted. You're the only one who hasn't."

"How do you know that?" Elle queried. "Who's had a go at you?"

"Nobody. I just said it must be an oversight."

"Nope…and you've just dropped yourself in it," Elle pointed out as Deb reddened. "Just remember Mum always said there was No El in Noel. That's me. You go and uphold the family honour. Tell them why I'm bah humbug. Remember, No Elle in Christmas."

"You know Mum didn't mean it as No Elle but as Noel in…oh, you know what I mean." Deb got up and did a turn of the cupboard Elle laughingly called an office. "Mum could be daft at times." She pointed an accusing finger at Elle. If a finger could be called accusing. "You need to wise up." She switched Elle's iPod on, and the tune *Santa Claus is Coming to Town* surrounded them.

Elle winced and lessened the volume from medium to low. It was way too early in the morning for her ears to be assaulted with Christmas music. Hadn't she decreased it once already for that very reason?

"As in, how wise up?" She moved out of the office, across the shop, and fiddled with three napkins rings with dancing elves on them and a teapot in the shape of Santa. Not her taste, but Deb adored it. Her twin loved all things Christmassy, which, considering Elle's bah humbug attitude was just as well. It made her dress the shop for the season. Otherwise, she might ignore it *and* not say why. "I'm savvy, thank you."

Deb, who had followed her, gave her the sort of look that, if she were a bloke, would wither his gonads. As she was female, it just gave Elle goosebumps. "Deb, enough. You attract the blokes, even if you won't do whatever is needed to attract the one you want. I don't, enough already. Been there, done that, crashed and burned, even before the t-shirt." She had no idea if that statement made sense or not to Deb, but to her it did. "You go and enjoy, and I'll stay at home and enjoy."

Deb scowled. "You could, too, you know, attract the blokes, and you have to go, you've been menti… Meant to."

And if that was what Deb had intended to say, Elle was a monkey's uncle.

"But I'm not interested…no, nor in women before you ask. I want to get established first and then I'll hunt me a fella again."

Deb coughed. "Er, Elle?"

"What?"

Deb's eyebrows lifted. "Customer," she mouthed.

Elle swivelled around and saw a customer…visitor…intruder…oh shit, a hot-as-Hades bloke who'd heard her proclamation.

One she knew. *Bugger. Cool it. Calm down and be smooth, civilised, and… argh…Shit, shit, and shit.*

"Well, good morning, Gus."

Deb did the sotto voce words thing again. "You know him?"

Elle scowled. Deb grinned.

Oh God, how pathetic.

"I didn't expect to see you today," she said in a tight, unwelcoming voice that grated on her ears. She cringed. What a god-awful attitude. However, she couldn't have changed it even if Santa appeared and said if she didn't she had to listen to Christmas music all year round. "I thought you'd swanned off to the other side of the world and forgot all about us boring people over here."

"Really?" the guy drawled in a knowing way. "I must be losing my touch." He did the gorgeous, sexy, aroused-and-love-you grin she'd learned to hate. "I thought you'd all be overjoyed to see me back and the wires would be hot with the news."

"Ohh," Elle mocked. "Don't we think a lot of ourselves? Nope, not interested enough to do that."

"Little cat," he said and laughed. "You never could lie worth a damn."

Elle glowered. "And you never could work out when your presence wasn't wanted."

Behind her, Deb appeared troubled, "Dunno who he is but, leave you to it. Remember murder is a criminal offence," she muttered under her breath. Or that was what Elle thought she'd mouthed. She nodded.

Sod it.

Elle smiled, or, she reckoned, grimaced in a very unwelcoming way at the bloke who now invaded her personal space. "I doubt you think you've lost it, so who am I to argue. We can agree to disagree." *As ever.* "So, what do you want? I don't have it, we're busy, nice to meet you once more, doubt we'll meet again, goodbye."

The music on her iPod changed to *Christmas Just Ain't Christmas Without the One You Love*, and the guy's lips twitched.

Sod him.

Chapter Two

Gus, *damn his eyes,* grinned and said, eyes crinkled up at the corners, "Ellie-mine, like I just said, you never could lie worth a penny. What the fuck is going on?"

Deb coughed. Elle jumped. She'd forgotten her twin was there, and Deb hated swearing.

"Language," she reminded Gus. "Others present."

"What?" he said, confused, and then appeared to notice Deb for the first time. "Hi, you must be…"

"On her way," Elle said hastily. "See you later, Deb."

"I, er, right, I'll be going," Deb said brightly. Too brightly—it promised a lot of need-to-know for later. "Speak soon. Remember to send the thing back."

"Fine," Elle said. "I'll interrogate you later as well. With thumbscrews, you turncoat." Leaving her alone, with *him*.

Deb laughed. "Nope. Bye, er, both of you." She disappeared in a hurry.

Rotter. Although she could well understand why Deb made her escape whilst she could.

Elle harrumphed and turned to the man who leaned on the wall next to the door, with his legs crossed at the ankle, looking for all the world as if he was where he wanted to be and totally at ease with whatever might happen.

Sod him again.

"To what do I owe this non-pleasure, Augustus? Can you make it snappy, I need to unpack some stuff and rearrange my Christmas gift table." She'd nearly said knicker drawer until she realised how that could sound, and how the bugger wouldn't take it as sarcasm but come up with some snarky comment.

"You only ever called me Augustus when you were pissed about something," he said in an innocent way. "What is it this time?"

"Your presence." Elle said pseudo-sweetly. 'As in, you here, not presents as a gift. So, why, what, and how long for? Oh, and thanks for calling, nothing to say, goodbye." She reached towards the gift table, which needed nothing doing to it, picked up a musical box circa 1930, and switched it on. The tinkly music was something she'd never heard before—or, she decided, ever wanted to again.

"For someone who's got nothing to say, you say an awful lot."

"Sod you." Argh, she sounded like a broken record, stuck on that one word.

"Still your favourite cuss word, my sweet?" He eased up from the wall and prowled around the shop.

"No, that is Augustus." Elle took a china jug from him and put it back down on a table. "Stop messing."

He grinned in appreciation of her comeback and then sobered. "It's Angus."

"What?" Elle swung around so fast she saw stars, and grabbed hold of the edge of the table for balance. "What's wrong with him?"

"Did I say anything was wrong?" Gus said in such an innocent voice, Elle itched to slap him. "I just said it was Angus, nothing else."

"Then what is Angus?" Elle said impatiently. "Why are you here and what does Angus have to do with your reason for being here?" There, that was succinct, was it not?

"Too much to say now," Gus replied. "When do you close for lunch?"

Close for lunch. What planet is he on? "I don't," Elle said shortly. The doorbell tinkled. "I have a customer, so…"

"So, I'd like the napkin rings, please." He picked the set of elf napkin rings up and handed them to her, and grinned.

Elle looked at them with distaste. Okay, they were probably fun and quirky, but not her thing.

Actually, these days, what about Christmas *was* her thing?

"Could you giftwrap them for me?"

What else could she say but, "Yes, of course."

Gus paid for his giftwrapped purchase and left the shop with a smile and what to her sounded like a veiled threat of 'see you later'.

As she had other customers, she couldn't say, 'not if I see you first', but she could think it. Instead, she smiled—fake, but she hoped convincing—and then ignored him to concentrate on a couple undecided whether they wanted a pretty dresser or not.

Thankfully, because she knew fine well they didn't get her full attention, they bought it and also some local pottery cups and saucers to go on it.

Several people browsed and didn't buy, several others did, and by four o'clock with her gift table half empty and her selection of napkins printed with Santa, robins, and holly in need of serious replenishment, she was ready to turn the open sign to closed and restock. Normally, she could do bits and bobs during the day, but she'd had no chance so far. She still couldn't get her head around why so many people felt the need to shop for Christmas, but when she saw the pile of sales slips, she definitely couldn't begrudge the habit. As long as she didn't have to join in. Her present list was short and succinct and comprised mainly of book tokens and restaurant vouchers.

She still hadn't RSVP'd to the invitation, though.

I've had no time.

She sent the same message to Deb when she texted in capitals: HAVE YOU SENT YOUR ACCEPTANCE YET!!!!!

She grinned at the *Hmmm* reply. If she carried on 'forgetting', would that get her out of going? She could only hope so.

Damn Gus, making her worried and not even giving her a hint about Angus. The old man was someone who had supported Elle through the bad times as well as the good, and someone she kept in touch with on a regular basis.

So why now did Gus feel it necessary to tell her Angus was worried? She'd last seen him the previous week, and he'd appeared in cracking form, and walked her off her feet as they did a circular tour along the river and back via the park and his bookies. He'd made no mention of worries, for himself or anyone else. She sent him a swift text: *Hey, what's up? Are you ok?*

There was no answer except for a thumbs-up and a heart. Which told her precisely nothing, but oh boy could she imagine.

Before she had the chance to lock the door, a young blushing lad of around fourteen or so came in, headed to a display of scarves, and sidled up to her with one of them and asked her if she thought his mum would like it.

"I'm sure she will," Elle said. "Would you like it in a gift box?" There was a sign behind her detailing the various costs.

The lad bit his lip. "Er, no thanks, it's fine." He took some notes out of his pocket. "Just the scarf. It's a birthday present."

Elle guessed he couldn't afford it. "Then let me wrap it for you." She found some silvery gold tissue and ribbon and ignored his agonised glance at the price list. "This is all part of the service if you are buying for you mum. I don't put that on the sign, though."

"Best not to," he said sagely. "Or you could be exploited."

"My exact thoughts." She tied the bow with nimble fingers and handed him a gift card. "There you go, all you need to do is write your message. And tell Mum if for any reason it's not what she wants, I'll change it. But I bet it's perfect, and she'll treasure it."

"I hope so," he said in a fervent tone. "Thanks, miss."

She smiled and nodded and followed him to the door, and flipped the sign ready to get the lock turned before any other latecomers got in. Not her usual modus operandi, but she was out of sorts and ready to go home and sink into a bath and a gin and tonic.

The music changed to an oldie she'd unearthed called *Grandma Got Run Over by a Reindeer*, just as the door was pushed and she automatically took a step back.

"Caught you." Gus shut the door behind him. "Shall I lock it?"

"With you on the other side? Yes please, I'm closed." Never mind Grandma, she felt as if *she'd* been run over, and not just by a reindeer.

'Tut, tut, Noelle, that's not very friendly. Fancy a drink?"

Elle rolled her eyes. "Augustus, read my lips. Tell me what's going on with Angus, and then I can tell you to bugger off. I'm tired, I'm hungry, and I'm heading for home. Alone."

Gus' eyes twinkled. "You never used to be so sarky."

"You never used to be such a pest. No, actually, scrub that, you did, but I ignored it."

"Ignore it again?" he suggested. "Easy."

"Not a chance. Now please, tell me why Angus is worried."

"Come for a drink and I will."

"Blackmail?" Elle said in a sugar-wouldn't-melt-in-her-mouth voice. "Beneath you, surely?"

"If you want to see it that way," he retaliated. "I prefer to see it as looking out for you. You're grey with fatigue, appear totally shattered, and I'm sure a drink and a packet of crisps would go down well." He cupped her face in his hands and kissed her swiftly before she could draw back. "Come on Ellie-mine, one drink and I'll see you home."

It was patently obvious she'd get nothing out of him if she didn't go. "Just one drink."

"Don't forget the crisps."

"And the bloody crisps," she snapped and cursed as he raised one eyebrow at her outburst. "Now amuse yourself while I cash up and get restocked."

He did it by tidying her shelves and humming to himself. "Where do you keep more pottery?"

Elle sighed. She'd lost her place in her column of sales. "In the stockroom, but you don't need to bother."

"I know." He disappeared into the stockroom and whistled, *Last Christmas*.

Of all the songs, it had to be that one.

Elle went back to her list.

Chapter Three

Ten minutes later, cash locked in the safe, she wandered out into the shop to look for him.

She found him in a corner sitting on the floor, reading a compendium of Christmas stories. As she approached, he glanced up. "I've got to have this, Ellie. Can I take it and you put the sale through tomorrow? Here." He handed her a tenner. "Put the change in the charity box."

"All one pence of it? Sure."

He laughed and passed over another note. "Add this to it."

"Thank you, I will." Elle put both notes in her pocket. "I'm ready."

He stood, clutching the book, and dusted himself off. "Don't sound so enthusiastic, I'll get a complex."

Heat rushed into her cheeks. "Sorry, as I said, I'm tired. Thank goodness we're closed tomorrow." She'd learned over time that Tuesday and Wednesday were slow days and chose to take them as well-earned R and R.

"Okay. Where's your coat?"

She gestured to the office.

"I'll get it, and your bag?"

"Thanks. And the carrier and the box next to it."

He blinked and nodded, to reappear a few minutes later laden down. "Good grief, were you going to carry all this yourself?"

Elle shook her head. "Nope, but as you're here and insist on following me home, I might as well use you."

"I might just change my mind," he grumbled.

"Then do it now, so I know not what to take."

Gus grinned. "Ah well, nice to know you think I'm good for something. After you."

She bit back a grin, determined not to let him see how much she liked him in this sort of carefree mood, then took her oversized tote from him before she unlocked the door and waited for him to go outside.

"Don't forget the alarm," Gus said and laughed.

She stuck her tongue out. "I'll forget you in a minute." Elle followed him outside and locked the door. "My mum would have said 'Don't teach your grandmother to suck eggs.'" An expression she never really understood, but in the circumstances appeared to fit. "I'm not the one who forgets to lock cars."

"Point taken, and it was only once."

'Three times, twice in a busy car park," Elle pointed out. "And you left your car keys on a wall once and…"

"Yes, okay," Gus butted in. "Red Lion or Blue Hare?" He named both the pubs in the village. "Be as busy as each other, I reckon."

"Blue Hare,' Elle said promptly. "Better gin." And less likely to run into any of her friends so early on. It tended not to be an early doors pub for people of their age as it was down a lane and easier to get to than the larger, more central Red Lion.

"Then lead on and let's get going. It's a bit nippy."

It would have made more sense to detour to her house one lane down, drop off her box and carrier, and go on unencumbered. However, Elle didn't trust either of them to actually get to the pub if that happened, her self-discipline was zilch when it came to him. One glance, one smile, and she was toast. Little did Deb know.

What a bloody shock her twin was going to get when Elle confessed all. She wasn't looking forward to it.

Plus, the thought of gin and tonic was a welcome one.

Gus elbowed the door of the pub open and nodded towards the well-named snug. It held four tables, and they were a tight fit. "See if you can grab somewhere to sit, and I'll order the drinks. What gin do you want?"

"That's daft. You go and dump the stuff, get the seats, and I'll order," Elle said. 'A pint of house ale?"

Gus scowled. "Do you have to argue all the time? I asked you to come."

She smiled sweetly. 'I said yes, I disagree when I think it is relevant or deserved. Like then. Do you have to snap back all the time? I was, *was,*" she emphasised, "trying to be helpful, not usurp your man position. You're laden; I thought it would make sense for you to put the packages down. I wasn't going to pay, just tell Pete you'd go up and give him the money, but hey ho, never mind." She swanned past him, entered the empty snug, and moved towards the table by the fire. He could sit comfortably, sweat, swear, or sod off. At that moment in time, she didn't much care which.

With exaggerated caution, Gus put the box on the floor, the carrier bag next to it, and stretched with his hands in the small of his back. Elle had a momentary pang of remorse. He'd offered to carry them when he had no idea how heavy they were. She could have said no or just asked for one or the other to come home with her, not both.

Why, whenever she was around Gus, did she let her temper get the better of her?

"Which gin?" he asked as he shrugged out of his coat. "Lime or lemon? Any preference of tonic? What flavour crisps?"

Elle scanned the lists of gins and pointed to one. "I'll have whatever is recommended with it, please. And smoky bacon crisps." She waited until Gus began to walk to the bar. "Gus?"

He turned with a look of query.

"Thank you."

He nodded and continued to the bar, where within a few seconds he was chatting and laughing with Pete, the landlord.

Elle shucked her coat and scarf and settled back on the old cushioned chair that had sat by the fire for as long as she could remember. Why couldn't she and Gus get on without sniping?

Too much baggage, and she didn't mean of the type he'd carried that evening for her.

The room was flooded with the sound of Slade singing *Merry Christmas Everybody*. Elle groaned and rolled her eyes. What next? *Santa Got Stuck up the Chimney?* That one gave her the heebie-jeebies.

Gus came back with her gin and tonic, a pint for him, and two packets of crisps held between his teeth.

"Did you ask for this?" she demanded. "My idea of hell?"

He did an innocent 'who me?' act. "Actually no, but I could have, after all, what's wrong with Christmas?"

"Everything," Elle said. "If I could sleep through it all, I would."

Gus shook his head in mock sorrow, sat beside her, and crossed one leg over the other. "Aww, bless you. You need to get into the spirit. It's magic."

"That's the last thing I need, No Elle in Christmas, remember? As for magic? Ha!"

"That's crap," he said forcefully. "You're just being negative for the sake of being ornery."

"Nope, not at all. Nothing good happens at Christmas." And if that didn't make her want to cry she didn't know what did.

"Nothing?" Gus asked in a quizzical way. "Not one thing?"

"Well, nothing that lasts," she temporised. "Now what is wrong with Angus?"

Gus sighed. "He's waiting for your RSVP."

Elle moved uneasily in her chair and took a sip of her drink to give herself time to think. "He knows I'm not going."

"By osmosis? Come on, Elle, you can do better than that, he *deserves* better than that."

That was true, but Gus was the last person she was going to give her reasons to. "I'll ring him in the morning."

"And say you'll be there, of course."

Only if Hell freezes over.

"I'll give the information to Angus."

"Oh, I can tell him for you," Gus said, all cheer and bonhomie. He took a long swig of his pint. "It would be my pleasure."

"I bet it would."

The door to the outside creaked. A young couple with a child of around five or six entered and sat on the opposite side of the room.

Damn, I forgot kids were allowed in until eight.

Elle put her glass down carefully. Just in case by holding it, she was tempted to throw the contents in his face, which she considered would be a waste of good gin. "Watch my lips," she said in a considered, slow and concise manner. "Not like that you…you…" She couldn't think of a word strong enough to dissuade him from showing her his aroused and annoying expression. Not a word which wouldn't get her slung out of the pub for unfriendly behaviour. Swearing in front of a child was a big no-no. Pete was hot on things like that. The Blue Hare prided itself on the exemplary reputation it rightly had.

"I...will...reply...to...Angus.   Tomorrow. Okay, now change the subject or I'll get up and go home." Elle downed her drink in a hurry. Bubbles went up her nose, and she spluttered. "Got it?" she asked once she was sure her speech would be coherent. Her glare should have sent shivers down his spine. To her annoyance, it didn't appear to faze him.

"I love you when you're angry," Gus murmured and took her hand in his. "Will you marry me?"

Chapter Four

E lle stared at him. "You *what*?"

He kissed her cheek, mainly because she turned her face at the last moment so he missed her mouth. "You heard," he murmured in her ear. "Will you marry me? Live with me and be my love. Grow old together and…"

"Start believing in fairy tales?" Elle said caustically. "In your dreams."

"Oh yes…along with you in my bed, in my arms, in my…"

She pushed him away. "All you, you, you, still, Gus. As ever. Where's the us, us, us?"

Gus stared at her. "It is us."

Elle shook her head. "Not how it sounds to me."

"You're overreacting due to words," Gus said in such a patient, talk-to-an-idiot voice she her clenched her fists. "It is all about us. Don't you think this stupidity has gone on long enough?"

"Stu... Stupidity?" Elle could hardly believe her ears. "Stupidity?" Her voice rose. "You egotistical, egocentric, egomaniacal moron. Go take a long walk off a short pier." She gave in to her temper, emptied her remaining drink, plus ice cubes over his head, grabbed her handbag and coat, and walked out, straight-backed and dignified.

The young boy's "wow" just as the music changed to *What Christmas Means to Me*, was funny enough for Elle to fight her instinct not to laugh out loud.

That summed it up perfectly.

It wasn't until she got indoors and realised she'd left the rest of her stuff in the pub that she burst into tears.

Five hours later, Elle was still fuming, even if it was after that long and hearty and supposedly healing bout of tears, which after the first self-pity-fest was mainly brought on by temper.

She looked at her face in the mirror and cringed. What a mess, and she didn't only mean her appearance. The whole night had been horrendous, and she couldn't deny her part in it all.

What next?

Elle washed her face, switched her phone back on, and sighed at the six missed calls and goodness knows how many messages. She stopped counting at eight. They could all wait until she'd made a coffee and a sandwich, sent a message to Angus to say she'd ring him tomorrow, and calmed down enough to face whatever was about to hit her.

She ate her sandwich—which tasted of sawdust not smoked ham—sipped at her coffee, and finally picked up her phone. Where to start?

The calls were from Gus, his number was etched in her brain, and no doubt Angus had given him hers—she'd not thought she'd need to ask him not to, and that would have resulted in a discussion she wasn't ready to have. Then, Angus himself—Deb, Deb, Pete from the pub, and Deb again.

Everyone had left a voice message. She tackled them in order. Gus' was short and terse. "When you get over your snit, get in touch with Angus. Don't worry, you can ask me next time. I might not say yes."

Sod him.

Deb's got increasingly worried. From "Who is he? What is he, what don't I know, ring me when you can," in the first one to "Ellie, are you okay? Pete's rung in a right tizzy," to the third, "If I don't hear by midnight, I'm calling the cops." Elle glanced at the clock and yelped. Five to twelve. She pressed Deb's number in a hurry. It was answered before she heard it ring.

"I'm okay, just pissed. Angry not drunk."

Deb's *whew* echoed around her. "But why didn't you answer your phone?"

"I turned it off to have a pity-fest. I needed it, but now I'm the spitting image of Morticia from the Addams family. Scary stuff."

"So who is he?"

Elle sighed. "Long story, I think I'd better tell you face to face."

"I'm on my…"

"Not tonight," she added hastily. "I'm off tomorrow, so are you, aren't you?" They usually took the same days off when possible, mainly so they got a chance to do things together. "Come here for lunch instead of us going into town." She didn't relish explaining to her twin, but at least it would give her a respite from all things Christmassy. Deb's idea of shopping would be to hit every outlet with decorations for sale and do her best to persuade Elle to buy them. Elle's idea was to refuse, every chance she got. It didn't always make for a good day out. Talk about chalk and cheese.

I didn't used to be like that.

"I'll bring the food," Deb said with a laugh. "You provide the gossip."

As Elle's idea of providing lunch was to beg Deb for the necessary goodies, it seemed fair enough to her. She could sort out just what gossip she'd share with her in the morning and make time to call Angus. Now she needed sleep.

"You're on. See you about one."

"Twelve," Deb said. "Gossip first, food later. Oh, and Pete rang me to say he had your box and bag of stuff. How and why?"

"All tied in with everything else, so tell you tomorrow." Elle ended the call and checked Pete's voice mail, which said just that.

Her messages were all variations on the themes of the voice mails.

Elle went to bed and expected not to sleep

The noise of something being dropped through her letterbox woke her a good eight hours later.

She'd slept like the proverbial log.

Yawning, she staggered downstairs and headed for the kitchen before she remembered the letterbox rattle. Well tough, coffee first, angst or whatever later. Elle turned on the radio and scowled as the much-too-cheery DJ announced a competition for the following week for the listeners to choose their favourite Christmas songs.

"It's November, for God's sake," Elle shouted at the radio. "Not December, not Christmas music, not for me." She switched over to a classical music station and prayed she wouldn't be assailed with carols. Thank goodness she wasn't. The gentle sounds of Eric Satie's *Gymnopédie Number One* suited her admittedly untutored and distinctly lacking of knowledge of all things musical, much better. Elle headed for the front door and picked up the envelope on the doormat.

No stamp, so hand-delivered.

She headed back to the kitchen and the coffee pot. Coffee was needed first, then she would tackle whatever was about to hit her.

Two coffees and a slice of toast later, she couldn't put it off any longer. She'd arranged for Angus to come and see her before she confronted Deb, and he was due in half an hour. Prior to that, she needed to get out of her PJs and into something slightly more respectable. Sponge Bob Square Pants PJ bottoms — courtesy of Deb a good ten years earlier — and a t-shirt with 'Sod Men' on it wasn't the look she needed to project.

After a swift shower, she dressed in jeans and an oversized jumper, her winter go-to days-off clothes, loaded the washing machine, switched it on, looked at the dust on her dresser, and blew at it and noted the time. She'd got ten minutes and couldn't put it off any longer.

The envelope had to be opened.

The flap was sealed but lifted with ease when she put the edge of a knife under it. She withdrew another envelope, this one unsealed. Inside that was a piece of card and a single sheet of paper.

The card was another invitation to the Christmas 'do', and the sheet of paper had four words written on it. 'Agree, for Angus' sake.'

No signature, but the writing was as familiar as her own.

Gus.

Why couldn't he go back to wherever he'd been for the last couple of years?

Where had he been?

She rolled that thought around her mind, the doorbell rang. She hurried to open it. "Right on…" She stopped speaking when she saw the two men on her doorstep. "Time," she finished.

One was Angus.

The other was Gus.

What the hell is he doing here?

She didn't have a chance to discover the answer before Angus spoke. "Noelle, you look amazing as ever." Angus, the only person who called her Noelle and got away with it, kissed her cheek and gave her a big hug. "Is that coffee I smell?"

She laughed. "Not yet, but it will be soon." She returned the kiss and the hug and glanced at Gus who shrugged.

"I'm the chauffeur today. Dad wants me to go and get some gravel, paint, and brushes. Too much for my car, so I offered to bring him. He won't drive my motor. I can't think why not."

"Not a chance," Angus said. 'Can you see me squeezing into the driver's seat and being able to get out in one move? I'd be rigwelted."

"You're the last person who would get stuck," Gus said. "And the first person I've known refuse to drive a Porsche."

'I'll stick to my Discovery, thanks," Angus said. 'Off you go, I'll phone when I need a lift."

It was Gus' turn to laugh. "I'm going. Have a good chat." He sketched a wave. Angus returned it and followed Elle indoors.

She shut the door and hung up Angus' coat. "Kitchen or lounge?"

"Kitchen. Then I can watch you make some Scotch pancakes to go with the coffee."

When he confessed he missed watching his wife bake, Elle started to make some sort of treat for them both while the coffee perked.

"I was going to cheat today," she said, and his face fell. "Only kidding," she added hastily as she put the coffee pot on the Aga and got the ingredients out for her pancakes. "Although I do have some fruit cake in the freezer for you. Deb made that, though. What are you painting?"

Angus settled himself in a chair. "Nothing, I just wanted to see your reaction when he dropped me off. Machiavellian, I know, but seriously, what is it with you two? I thought you got on okay with my son when he was around last time. For six months or so you seemed inseparable, and then wham. I went on holiday, and when I came back three weeks later, he's gone off to New Zealand and you're walking about like someone had taken your savings and left you a penny." He studied her thoughtfully. "Or taken your future?"

Chapter Five

That was going for the jugular with a vengeance. Elle weighed out her ingredients *and* weighed up her words carefully before she spoke.

"What has Gus told you?"

"Bugger all," Angus said cheerfully. He poured out two mugs of coffee and added milk. "And as I'm a nosy sod, and two of my favourite people appear to be at odds with each other, I want to know why. All Gus says is that it's up to the two of you to sort things and to keep my nose out of it." He sounded disgusted. "So I thought I'd try you instead."

Elle grinned. "I won't put it in quite such a rude way, but I agree with Gus. It's up to us to decide if we can be friends again." Something she was not at all sure about.

Angus made a noise akin to a steaming kettle. "You're as bad as him. Right then, I'll sulk and plot later. Where's the RSVP to the Christmas bash?" He began to whistle *Jingle Bells*. "Trust you to forget. Gus reminded me I said I hadn't received one. I'd take it as read, but the committee said they wanted every yes in writing." He paused. "And every no."

Elle flipped her pancakes with casual expertise. They were the one thing she could cook—along with fairy cakes—which she didn't have to concentrate on. "Angus, I did say I'm not that much into Christmas. Never have been." *And even less these days.* "My mum used to say I was the No El in Noelle and totally misnamed. Pantomimes freaked me out, still do. All that leg slapping and innuendo you're supposed to find funny. I hated having to open presents and be pleased with something I didn't want, and write polite, untrue thank you notes. Santa scared me, I couldn't see the point of standing in the cold to sing, and lots of nasty things happened at that time of year." She took a deep breath. "Believe me, I'm better off on my own. Several days of me, me, and recharge-my-batteries me."

Angus whistled long and loud. "Wow. You are bah humbug about it, aren't you?"

She shrugged. "Yup. Ma says it's my hibernation time, Deb says it's my miserable sod time, and Gu... Generally, they're correct," she improvised hastily. "Honestly, Angus, I can't think of anything I'd like less, and that includes red liquorice and root canal treatment. Please, just accept my apologies, will you?"

He sighed. "Write it out. I think you're wrong, you'll be the only one not there. Look as if it's beneath you and all that."

"Have you been speaking to Deb?" Elle asked with suspicion. It was almost the same reply as her twin had said.

Gus opened his eyes wide. "Why do you say that?" he said in a fake-innocent way. He spoiled it by adding a wheezy laugh. "She may have mentioned you weren't keen."

"I'm not." Elle sighed. "Say I'm going if you want. I'll just cry off nearer the time."

Angus shook his head in sorrow. "It's not right for a young lass like you to be so negative."

Maybe not, but I do have reason.

"Eat your pancakes." She put three on a plate, handed him maple syrup and blueberries, and sat across the table. "I broke my arm at Christmas, my cat ate my hamster at Christmas, Mum's mum forgot to come for dinner, and we ate at seven instead of three, I chipped a front tooth at Christmas, and found and lost someone I liked at Christmas. So many bad memories." *Actually like is a misnomer, but... I will not go there.*

Angus patted her arm. "There now, I had no idea it was so bad. You do the yes, and we'll find a reason to change it to no later, if you really want to."

"Thanks, Angus." She kissed his cheek. "Much appreciated."

He nodded. "Right, now that's done and dusted, you and Gus."

He was like a stuck record.

"There is no me and Gus," Elle said emphatically. Too emphatically, as Angus's eyebrows disappeared to where his hairline would be—if he had any hair. "We were...friends for a while and then we weren't. He went to wherever he went, and I stayed here." The bare unvarnished truth. "I have neither heard from him nor seen him for ages until he popped up yesterday."

"Like a bad penny?" Angus asked.

"Just like. I'm sorry, Angus, but don't go trying to play matchmaker or whatever, because there's nothing to match." Or make. "Our short friendship was over and done with a long while ago." *One year, ten months, and…*

"Pity," Angus broke into her gloomy thoughts as he hummed a few bars of *Lonely This Christmas*.

Elle rolled her eyes.

"Enough, Angus. It will not. You'll have Gus, and I'll…be fine. Plus, I've promised Deb I'll…" Her mind went blank. What the hell had she promised Deb? "To share the cooking of our Christmas dinner," she finished.

"So you'll spend the day with your sister then?"

Elle crossed her fingers behind her back. "Yup." In fact, she had no intention of doing anything of the sort. She hoped by then Deb would be hooked up with Oscar Prenderville and cosied up to him over dinner. That thought gave her a momentary pang of loneliness, but she squashed it. She was gregarious enough the rest of the year; her few days of unsociable behaviour could surely be overlooked?

But it's not just a few days, is it, her conscience nagged. *You've started already.*

It was handy the 'do' was in the first week of December. It gave her time to plot before then and Oscar time to plot after.

"I'm making the trifle and the smoked salmon mousse." That was at least true.

Angus appeared sceptical. "If you say so. Right." He finished his coffee, which must have been stone cold. "Tick the 'yes' box on your invite, and I'll pass it over."

Elle picked up the new non-dog-eared invitation and ticked the box. She handed it to Angus who scrutinised it and nodded.

"That's my girl."

"Mind you, I'm not going," Elle warned him. "So don't get your hopes up."

"All right, I get the message." Angus stood and glanced around. "Where's my…ah, there it is." He lifted his phone. "Better text the boss."

"I can run you home," Elle said. Anything rather than Gus there again. "It's no problem."

"Don't you go putting yourself out," Angus said. "He'll be mooching around town anyway, catching up." He sent a brief text and a few seconds later got a reply. "Ten minutes. Did you know he's looking for a house and premises to work in?"

Her stomach churned. Wasn't it bad enough to have him around for a short while, upsetting her equilibrium, let alone for good?

"No," Elle said shortly and realised how abrupt and snarky she sounded. "That'll be nice for you. Not going to share a house then?' She grinned. "Or would that put paid to Mrs Govern bringing you shepherd's pie and your sneaky cigars?"

Angus tutted. "Sneaky? Who says my cigars are sneaky?"

"Well, aren't they?" Elle winked.

He snorted.

"The cigars aren't, the fact I smoke them up the top of the garden or blow the smoke out of the window probably is. We'd end up nagging each other to death. Him and his only green apples not red, nothing fried, and brown rice not white. I've not had a fried egg since he got home. Not that I have many anyway, I do take care of myself whatever Gus thinks to the contrary, but now I yearn for one. Forbidden fruits and all that. I mean seriously, what man says things like that?"

"One who gets a rise out of his dad, I would think."

Angus appeared struck by that remark. "Clever devil. I'll show him."

Elle chuckled. "I bet you will." There was the noise of a car approaching, and then an engine switched off. "That sounds like him now." She headed towards the door.

Angus followed her. "Here's your hat, nice to see you, goodbye?"

"What? Oh lord, no." She realised how her actions must appear. "I didn't want him to have to get out and knock on the door, and I'm meeting Deb soon."

"It wouldn't kill him." Gus pulled her in for a hug. "Whatever went wrong between you two, neither of you give the impression of being very happy about it. Why not give each other another chance? Or at least talk about the whys and wherefores. And that," he finished in a rush as the doorbell rang, 'is the last I'll say on the subject, except don't cut off your nose to spite your face, and who are you actually punishing with your nothing-to-do-with-Christmas attitude? Will you be round next week to go to the pub to play dominoes? We need to win."

The monthly domino tournament was a hard-fought competition. They were lying in third.

"Definitely."

"And you don't drive, so we can celebrate our victory," Gus said. The doorbell rang again. "Impatient, little b, eh?"

As ever.

She steeled herself to open the door to him, and then had to tamp down the massive disappointment when he merely nodded and escorted his dad to the car.

She had asked for it, but it bloody hurt.

That and Angus' pointed words had driven home.

Just who *was* she punishing?

Chapter Six

Elle tidied up in a desultory manner, her mind not really into upsetting dust bunnies—who would just regroup in greater numbers, no doubt—and set to emptying the tumble drier instead. To take her mind off the mundane task, she pondered her intransigent attitude towards all things Christmassy.

Yes, she mused, as she folded towels and put them in the airing cupboard, lots of little unpleasant-at-the-time things happened around Christmas when she was a child, but should they seriously affect her now? Was it not time to grow a pair, or pull up her big girl panties, build a bridge, and get over it and all those stupid sayings that basically intimated you were being daft and or childish. She slammed the airing cupboard door with a satisfying thump, and glared at the vacuum cleaner, which glared back accusingly.

"No way, Jose, not today. Today is a blow-the-dust, ignore-the-dirt, and cope-with-life day. Argh, now I'm talking to a bloody hoover." At least it couldn't answer back. "Crazy."

She reckoned if she was completely honest with herself, crazy was an understatement. As was daft and childish. Why should the fact her hamster died and she broke her arm mean that Christmas was a no go? Why not go ahead and make new, better memories? Learn to, if not love all things Christmas, not hate them. Roll with them, find things she could stand, and maybe even like a lot, and let silly niggles be beneath her.

Learn to forgive?

That might not be so easy.

Go on, give it a go. Be brave. She imagined Angus saying that to her, and then winking in the way he did when he dared her. The last time she'd tried to bowl in an impromptu cricket match between the two of them, she'd broken the window of his greenhouse. He'd roared with laughter and said it was his own fault as he'd goaded her into doing it. Now she imagined she could hear him goading her to get on with it, just do it.

Maybe. In a defiant mood, she turned the radio on and then three seconds later wished she hadn't. It was the Golden Oldies hour, and Dean Martin was singing *I've Got My Love to Keep Me Warm*. She bit her lip.

He'd sung that when... Enough. She changed stations.

This time it was even worse. *All I Want for Christmas is You* was almost at the end, and it was followed by *Merry Christmas Baby*.

This 'suck it up buttercup' wasn't going to be that easy. She glowered at a pile of ironing and shoved it in the airing cupboard. Enough was enough. She'd make some biscuits instead. Comfort food and not quite as fattening as her other go-to. Cream and fruit meringues with extra sugar!

When *It's Gonna be a Cold, Cold, Christmas* blasted out from the radio, she switched it off and burst into tears.

Been there, done that, and got the t-shirt.

The doorbell rang, and she looked at the grandfather clock she'd bought when she'd purchased the house. Too big, impractical, took a lot of time and attention to keep it as it should be, and she loved it.

How come Deb was so early? Her phone signalled a text message from Deb: *Can't do today, can we do tomorrow???*

She sent a swift thumbs-up and 'speak later', ran down the stairs, and flung the door open. A bit stupid if it was someone ready to do mischief.

She hoped the bloke standing there didn't have that in mind.

Then she took a step back, which opened the door even wider as if in invitation.

"You're ea...not expected," she said stupidly as Gus took a step forward and accepted the unwitting invite. "What are you doing here?"

"I've come to sort this mess out," Gus said, and once Elle closed the door, he put his jacket over the newel post and his scarf on top. "To try to say why I did what I did, discover why you did what you did." He paused and hugged her, before he rested his chin on the top of her head. "To see if we can find a way out of this mess."

Elle sighed, all her antagonism dissolved by his earnest tone. "Do you honestly think we can? So much has gone on...so much time passed."

"So much not thinking of each other?" he asked. "Not on my part. I've thought of you very day, even before I came home. Can we sit and talk? Really openly and honestly talk?"

It was up to her.

"I'd like that," Elle said softly. "Really like that. Funny, I was due to spend the day with Deb, but she's cried off."

"Really?" Gus tried for an innocent look and didn't quite make it.

"Your doing?"

He nodded. "Sort of. Dad's actually. He had a go at me, like he said he'd had a go at you. Suggested I asked Deb to give me a few hours to chat to you, and then I was sure you'd talk to her. Deb came back with 'have today'." He shrugged. "So here I am."

Elle thought she might have words with her twin later, and she hoped they would be good ones.

"Then let's get comfortable and you can begin."

It was one thing saying that, another to know whether she should start or sit back and let Gus talk. Elle made coffee with the thought she was awash with the stuff. Thank goodness she'd gone for decaff or her nerves would be shot. She carried the tray into the lounge, let Gus do the polite thing and take it from her, and waved to the pancakes. "Left over from your dad's visit. Sorry there's not much else. Deb is the baker, not me."

Gus laughed. He took one and accepted his coffee. "I remember. Pancakes and crepes, lemon and sugar, not orange and honey."

"I don't do many crepes these days but I have learned how to make decent fairy cakes and digestive biscuits. Which has nothing to do with us and the here and now."

"True, but put me down for some of both of them if and when you bake." Gus inclined his head, swallowed half his coffee in two large gulps, and put his mug down. "I miss you Ellie-mine," he said earnestly, pulled her closer, and held her firm against him. "Oh so very much.

Every minute of every day. The light has gone out of my life, and I'm lost. I'm missing something so important it's akin to a physical pain. I know I was a twat, a total eejit, but I was a typical bloke. Immature and like a kid in a sweet shop. I wanted everything my way, didn't consider there were two sides to every story and discussion. I think I've grown up, but there's one thing I still do want."

She looked at him in query as he stroked her hair, her cheek and her neck.

"I want Ellie-mine, though I can't demand, just beg. He touched his fingers to her lips and then pressed them to his own. Smiled and sighed. "I really do want."

"What's that?' she said quietly, hardly daring to think what the answer might be.

"That's the easiest thing I've ever had to answer. I still want you, Ellie-mine, I still yearn for you. You are my sun, my moon, and my stars. My reason for living." His voice dropped and softened. "My all." The hand he'd placed on her shoulder tightened before it appeared he had to consciously relax it. "If nothing else, believe that."

Oh, I do. Why I don't know, but…

Elle threw caution to the wind. "I feel the same." Whatever might happen later, she knew what she wanted to happen now. "Take me to bed, please, Gus. Take me now and make love with me. Let's forget about our problems and what-if or what might have been. Let's live for now. Make love with me."

"I thought you'd never ask." He stood and very unromantically put her in a fireman's lift. "Show me the way."

She giggled, and he patted her bum.

"To the bedroom, Ellie-mine. I reckon I'll fumble through it after that."

Chapter Seven

"If that's fumbling," Elle said dreamily an hour or so later, "heaven help me when you know what you're doing." She traced a whorl of his chest hair around one hard nipple, found the nub, and pinched it non-too-gently. "I'm absolutely exhausted."

Gus nibbled her ear. "Nah, you're not, you're recovering fast."

Elle rolled over onto her stomach to stare at him. "I am?"

"Oh yes," he confirmed. "Just about fully recovered and ready to make a cuppa."

"You reckon?"

He patted her bum again, a habit of his she'd forgotten.

Elle wriggled. "Oy, enough."

"A cuppa while I go all over manly, and no, not stop in bed and doing the lording 'I'll stay here' thing, whilst the little woman scurries around. I'll get dressed, go downstairs, and stir the fire up." Gus stretched, and the duvet slipped down to his groin. "Then I'll do the lording thing and drink my cuppa, while you do whatever you need to do." He moved, and the duvet went even lower. Almost…

Elle's mouth went dry. If he stayed like that for many more seconds it wouldn't only be the fire downstairs that got stirred up. Even after their lovemaking and the once long-forgotten but now well-remembered delicious aches and pains in places she'd not had them for…well, since the last time she'd made love with Gus, she still felt tingles down her spine as she took her fill. How on earth had she managed these last couple of years without him?

With difficulty. And closing her mind to all things Gus. She watched him head for the bathroom across the hall, raced into the en suite, and within ten minutes had washed, dressed, and made her way downstairs.

He followed a few minutes later, whistling cheerfully. Elle recognised the tune and grinned to herself. *Cavatina*—he was beautiful—which he used to sing to her by changing he to she and was to is.

He appeared in the kitchen a few moments later. "Nice blaze going," he said, "and the room is warm." He accepted the cup of coffee and thick doorstep of a ham sandwich Elle handed him. "Ta, hon. Shall we sit and then spill our guts? Metaphorically, of course?"

"You have such a way with words," Elle said, resigned to the heart-to-heart she was dreading. "Yes, let's." *And get it over with.*

"I'll start," Gus said once they were seated side by side. He had his arm along the back of the sofa and stroked the tips of her hair with his fingers. "By saying I was a self-centred, unfeeling, unthinking bastard. Actually, not quite right. I did think. Of myself. I didn't take into account what you had going on, or your feelings. For all it's worth, I'm sorry. If I'm honest I was sorry almost straight away but too pig-headed to say so. All I saw was a marvellous opportunity for me in New Zealand, and didn't think about the fact you'd just taken the lease of the shop on, and might not be so keen to up sticks as I was. So when you said you couldn't, I thought, well, I can, and I did. I missed you, but pure bloody-mindedness wouldn't let me say I was wrong or I missed you. I wrote, but your answer was stilted. Dad said whatever had happened between us, I was an idiot. You had a haunted look in your eyes, and I sounded unhappy. I texted Dad who said, well, I won't repeat it word for word, but I got the idea. So I served my contract, learned a lot, and made arrangements to come home and set up a business here. Hoped you'd see me, let me explain and apologise and take it from there."

He half smiled. "I love you, Elle, always have and always will."

Elle bit her lip. If only it were that easy. "I love you," she said slowly. "But you hurt me. You showed me that what I did meant nothing to you or to us. It was 'if you loved me, you'd not even need to think about it'. You assumed it was just the shop, and in your words, I could always get another one. Which, of course, I could. But I'd signed a contract and been given the shop by people who put their faith in me. One of whom was your dad. No way could I let them down. It was only for six months at first, but you wouldn't even listen to me say I'd get out of it then. Your words were now or never. So…" She shrugged. "You know the rest."

"I don't know the ending, though," Gus said.

Elle sighed. "Nor do I. When you didn't come back, I took a three-year contract on the shop. And though I was determined not to say this, my dad's not been too well. He's on the mend now, and Mum and Dad are off on a cruise, but at the time it was one more added worry."

Gus kissed her. "And I was too wrapped up in my opportunity to listen. I'm listening now."

The problem was, Elle didn't know how to discuss all the things she wanted to know and understand. Plus, and it was a very big plus, she wasn't the girl she was then, and she was damned sure he wasn't the guy she'd known.

How to explain that and not sound arsy?

"I don't know where to start, Gus. We've grown up. I'm not the young girl who jumped into love and was knocked back so cruelly."

He nodded. "Shall I woo you? Come a courtin'?"

"I'd like that."

"Then, Ellie-mine, my life, my love, will you marry me?"

Again?

"If that's your idea of courting, Augustus, it's pitiful." Elle pushed him, and he fell onto the floor, laughing like a loon.

"I know," he gasped, "but I couldn't resist it. You should see your face, love. Confused doesn't even half cover it."

"I should think not," Elle said with dignity. "You know it's impossible."

"Maybe, maybe not." He got off the floor. "Next question, do I stay or do I go now?" He whistled a few bars of the song and then changed to *Take Me I'm Yours*. "Dad's over in town for the night, not that he'd mind, but I don't want him to get ideas of things we haven't got to, if you know what I mean?"

Elle nodded. There were a lot of things to cover before they got to the being together stage again.

If they ever did. Until then, she hadn't realised how wary she'd become.

However. "Stay," she said. "And start your courting."

He tilted his head in query "Any ideas how?"

"Cook dinner?" she said hopefully.

He burst out laughing. "Curry?"

"The way to my heart is via a good curry. Sounds perfect."

"Then lead me to your store cupboard."

Gus was loud in admiration of the well-stocked pantry she had, not so much when he saw the sell-by dates on most of the items there. "You do know spices lose their heat as time goes by?" he said as he sniffed a tin of turmeric with a use-by date of three years previous.

"I don't keep anything that smells iffy," Elle said. "In my defence, I hardly ever use them and so I guess that's why. Anyway, will it do, or do I need to make a mad dash to the shop before it shuts?"

"I'll make it do." Gus opened and sniffed three more tins, said they weren't too bad in a grudging manner, and lined them up on the counter. "What have we got to go in the curry?"

Elle thought rapidly about the contents of her fridge and larder. "Um, diced lamb, chicken, cauli, potatoes, peas, rice…"

"Okay, I'll sort something. All fresh?"

"Well, none of that sort of food is out of date," Elle said, indignant that he might entertain notions along those lines. Then she realised what he meant. "Nothing frozen."

Gus nodded and glanced at the radio. "Can we have it on?"

Elle turned the switch and beamed as non-Christmas music played. She might be getting her head around Christmas, but softly-softly was a better approach than full-on everything.

"Dad says you're anti Christmas," Gus said. He sliced onions in a way that Elle would have chopped her finger off instead of the vegetable if she'd tried it. "My fault?"

"Partly," she said. Honesty was always the best way to go. "All our major happenings were around then. We met at Christmas, we, well, you know, at Christmas, you left at Christmas."

Gus winced. "So let's get married at Christmas and…ouch, okay, enough already. I'll shut up now."

Elle had nipped his ear.

She smiled. "Exactly. We cannot get married, all right?"

He sighed. "I think we could but I won't push it yet." He put the onions to one side and began to dice the chicken.

Elle admired his deftness and decided she was happy not being able to cook like him. There seemed an awful lot of preparation before you got to eat the fruits of your labour.

"Is it all my fault?" Gus asked. "I've screwed your life up and made you a bah humbug person?"

"Not all yours," Elle said. She strove to be honest. It wasn't easy. "Lots of silly niggly things from when I was a kid. But I've vowed to ignore them. I realised I wasn't just upsetting other people, I was upsetting myself as well. I'm going to embrace a bit of Christmas spirit."

"With that in mind," Gus said with a grin as he continued with his cooking and the aroma of spices filled the kitchen, "mine's gin, and I'm happy not to wait until Christmas. Where's the garlic?"

Elle handed him a jar. He shook his head in sorrow, and she didn't think he was making it up.

"How can you use this when you can get nice plump proper cloves?"

She grinned. "Because I'm not a chef. But I do have proper lemon for the G and T."

"There's hope for you yet."

The teasing, happier conversations set the tone for the evening.

The hot-and-sweaty loving set the tone for the night.

The next morning, Elle cooked bacon and eggs, something she could do reasonably well, and even remembered to sauté some mushrooms to go with it.

Gus made a restocking of her cupboard list. His treat to both of them, he said, as he hoped he'd be cooking a lot more of their meals in the future.

Elle turned the bacon and remembered something she'd pondered over when she woke in the wee small hours whilst Gus slumbered beside her.

"What shall I tell Deb when I see her later? And what will you say to Angus?"

"That they're both invited for dinner asap. And we'll do our explanations then?" Gus suggested. "You can ring your parents, or email as well?"

"All the explanations, and I don't know the answers," Elle said.

"That we're taking it day by day until you agree to marry me...?" He ducked the tea towel she flung at him and laughed. "Sorry, hon, couldn't resist."

"I'll go back to bah humbug again," Elle warned. "You know we can't get married."

"No I don't, give me one good reason why?"

She stared at him as if he'd grown two heads "Sorry? Reason why what?"

"Why we can't get married."

"Because," she said patiently, as if she was talking to a two year old, "we're both married already."

"Ah, you have a point."

Chapter Eight

An hour later, Gus left to head for his solicitor's to sign the deed of sale for his new premises. He'd hoped, he said, to take Elle to see them before he did so, but a swift session on the stairs put paid to that.

"Show you it as soon as I can," he said. He kissed her and almost put his departure back another hour. "Good luck with Deb."

They'd managed to discuss how much Elle should share, and Elle was adamant she needed to tell Deb while they were alone.

"I'll holler if I need you."

Gus was going to speak to his father as well. "If I'm not needed earlier, ring me when the coast is clear. I'll cook. But first, oh yes, mmm…"

Elle pushed him out of the door as his hands moved to her breasts. "We do not have time, Gus. You're almost late already. Shoo." She took his hands, moved them behind his back, and grinned. "But hold that thought."

"Insatiable woman. I love it. See you later. Love you." He disappeared at a run.

It was like London buses, nothing for ages and then lots…not that she was complaining, Elle thought. Though her back would later. The stair edges were sharp when you rolled around on them.

She'd never be able to look at the stair runner in the same way again. When her phone rang, Elle cussed. She was halfway through tidying the earthquake, normally called her bedroom, a job she hated.

It was Deb. "Morning, sis, I'm running late, as in mega late. Fancy meeting me in the shopping centre?"

Small but well-equipped, it ran a free bus service four times a day from outside Chandler's

Mall. As much as she wanted to say 'no, not really', when she knew she was due the third degree, Elle noticed there was a bus in half an hour.

"Okay, why not," she replied in the affirmative and rushed to find her outdoor clothing and crossbody bag. She had a couple of birthday presents to buy—one being for Angus—and could do with a new pair of warm gloves. Her present pair sported a hole on one thumb, which she'd sewn up several times. Christmas gifts would have to wait until she thought about what for whom.

Deb met her at the bus stop and towed her into the centre.

From every speaker, Christmas songs blared out. Elle winced. She should have realised. "Did you do this on purpose to make me even more miserable?" she asked, in keeping with her rapidly disappearing hate-the-season persona. They dodged three giggling teens, a bloke on a skateboard, and two old ladies who stood gossiping and blocked three quarters of the pavement. "Joke," she added in a rush when she saw Deb's hurt expression. "I hadn't realised it would be so busy."

"Special sale day," Deb replied. "Now I'm back home from Italy I'm doing every Scottish thing possible. Even down to a tartan-dressed angel for the tree. I'm after some other bits and bobs for the day I promised not to mention as well. And a dress, ditto."

Elle took a deep breath. "You can mention it, just don't shove it down my throat. And, er, tell me what you'd like for your present."

Deb dropped her bag in surprise. She picked it up as she stared at her twin. "Say again."

"Don't push your luck,' Elle warned. "Or I might regress."

"In that case, a new makeup bag, some caramels, a book token, and a surprise, as in, my sister back," Deb said rapidly. "Though I reckon I've just had that. I need a drink. Let's nip into the Blue Hare on the way home. Let's go now, come on, we'll get a taxi."

"No way, you promised me shopping, so shopping I need. I have a list."

"A Christmas list?" Deb asked with amazement. "Are you a doppelganger of my twin? A changeling." She pinched Elle who squirmed.

"Cut it out, or I'll tickle you."

"Definitely my twin, and Christmas list."

"Well, no," Elle replied, as apologetic as she could be under the circumstances. She urged Deb on towards a posh undies shop. Elle decided she needed fancy knickers and refused to dwell on why. "But a list nonetheless. And there *is* Bl…er, blimey, Christmas music on. Though please God, not *When Santa Got Stuck Up the Chimney* again. That did give me nightmares as a kid once I realised the Santa at the village Christmas Fayre was Uncle Stan. I still get nasty goosebumps whenever I hear it."

Deb stopped dead. "You never told me that?"

"What, Uncle Stan or my worry he'd get stuck in our chimney?"

"Both. Poor Ellie, you did have a lot of anti-Christmas thoughts, didn't you. And no wonder. But…" Deb tilted her head to one side. "You're a big grown up girl now…well, most of you."

They both burst out laughing. Deb did a semi-downward glance at Elle's admittedly neat and not very ample bosom, and then at her own more rounded figure.

"Some of me is more grown up than the rest," Elle admitted. "Now I'm after some new undies."

"Ohhh, why?"

Elle mimed a zipping motion. "Nosy."

"Too true. And I haven't forgotten you need to tell me all about you-know-who and you."

Elle mocked groaned. Or half mocked. "Okay, Miss Nag, but not here. Let's shop, grab a top-notch takeout, and we'll chat at home. Anything I say will be for your ears only." She walked to the door of the posh knicker shop, stopped dead, and blinked.

What the hell is he doing in there? Gus stood at the counter chatting to the assistant whilst she wrapped something up. Luckily, his back was towards them.

"I've changed my mind," she muttered to Deb. "Let's go to the pub."

"But I thought you wanted knickers?"

"Later. I, er, need a wee, and we might as well have a drink at the same time. Well, not the same time, but you know what I mean."

Poor Deb appeared as if Elle had lost her mind, and no wonder, Elle thought. Talk about about-turns; she'd done more than her fair share that day. "I'll explain in a sec," Elle said. She dragged Deb a few steps away from the doorway. "Oh shit, too late."

Whilst they'd been talking, Gus had exited the shop and stopped next to them.

"Fancy meeting you here," he said to Elle. "Off to get something to tickle my fancy?"

"Itching powder?" she retorted. "If you like."

He roared with laughter and turned to Deb. "She's ever the wag."

Deb looked bemused. "She is?"

He nodded. "Oh yes, even if you don't realise it." He put the parcel he held into Elle's hands. "This is for you, you might as well have it now. Oh, and dress wise. I'm partial to sort of swirly patterns and a mix of blues and greens."

Elle stared at the parcel as if it were dynamite. Beside her, Deb chuckled, and the DJ over the tannoy announced it was time for *Mistletoe and Wine*.

What next?

"I prefer red or yellow," Elle said, lying through her teeth. Neither colour did her any favours, and he knew fine well the colours he mentioned were also her favourites and suited her. "And actually, not in the market for a new dress."

"Oh, you've got one for the do then?" Gus said, all innocence. "Angus said you promised to go.

I'll pick you up, of course. Oh, and don't forget tomorrow night."

"Did he?" Angus never said such a thing, she was sure, and there was no 'of course' about it. "Tomorrow?"

"Our date."

"We do not have a date." Not that sort of date, anyway. They'd reverted to the see you later, casual, take-it-as-read sort of dates. Nothing planned per se, but she knew he'd be round later on and…

Deb coughed, and Elle jumped.

"Oops, woolgathering."

"I must have forgotten to ask you," Gus answered in a butter-wouldn't-melt-in-his-mouth voice. "Take it as asked."

Elle itched to slap him. He was teasing her when, with Deb staring from one to the other, he knew she couldn't retaliate.

"Never mind, I'll still pick you up at eight," he added and winked.

"Washing my hair."

He laughed. "I'll dry it for you."

Like you did before and we both ended up soaked?

The wicked expression on his face showed her he'd remembered that as well.

"Sorry," Elle said. Her cheeks heated. "Got to dash or we'll miss the bus."

She gave Deb a pleading glance, which her twin picked up on at once.

"Sheesh, yeah, nice to have met you er, yes, right, bye." She let herself be towed away towards the bus stop.

"There's no bloody bus for ages," Deb said as soon as they were out of earshot. "What if he knows that?"

"I'll plead ignorance."

"Okay, okay," Deb panted. "Slow down, please, I'm about ready to have a heart attack or something."

"Okay." Elle risked a quick peek behind them to see Gus, standing where they had left him, a picture of a man with no guile in him until he winked. *Damn the man.*

"I need explanations, sis. Lots of them."

"I know." Elle steered them to the taxi rank, opened the door, and gave her address. "Explanations, a curry or a sarnie, a glass of vino, and a lot of mea culpa on my side. I hope I have tissues."

"For me?" Deb asked.

"Nope, for me. I'm getting teary as I think of it, and no, I'm not sure if it's from temper or sadness for what almost was." *And high fives for what I hope is now?*

"Clear as mud again," Deb said. "But as I guess the giver of presents and partial to your favourite colours plays a bigger part than I know or could guess, I'm all ears."

The taxi drew to a halt. Elle paid off the driver, and once they were indoors turned to Deb. "You get the wine, I'll light the fire and get some food."

"And then I'll get some answers," Deb replied.

"And then you'll get some answers."

Chapter Nine

"Right, I'm all ears again." Deb wriggled deeper into the seat cushion of the settee. "You, Gus, Angus, what?"

Elle put three lumps of coal and a log on the fire and watched it flare up nicely. The room was warm, but the fire added comfort to it. Every little thing helped.

She chose her words carefully. She didn't want to show Gus in too horrendous a light, but she did intend to show how hurt she'd been. Luckily,

with the senses they had as twins, she guessed—
hoped—Deb would read between the lines.

"When you went to Italy to learn your posh-
nosh cooking, I met Gus. He'd come from New
Zealand to meet up with his dad."

Deb rolled her eyes and snorted. "Posh nosh
indeed."

Elle mock glared. "Do you want to hear about
this or not?" Half of her hoped that Deb would
say 'not'. The other, more realistic half accepted
she had to share.

"Of course I do. Go on. He came home to meet
up with his dad. How do you mean?"

"Gus went away to do a gap year, and this was
him coming home. Seven years later."

Deb snorted. "Some gap year."

Elle inclined her head. "As you say. Anyhow,
we met, we got together, and we fell in love. Or
so we thought. Several months later, he got a
chance to go back to New Zealand to work for a
very prestigious chef…yeah, another great cook
in the vicinity."

"I think it sounds as if Gus is more than a
cook," Deb said with a laugh. "But I get the idea.
Hold on… He went?"

Elle nodded. "And wanted me to go with him. I said no."

Deb opened her eyes as wide as she could and gasped. "You...said no? And you loved him?"

Elle got the familiar, horrible sensations of loss and despair she'd experienced so often in the first few months after Gus had left. The wondering what else she could have done. The hatred of the stilted emails she'd written to him and he answered in the same way. The tears when he made no mention of if or when he'd come back to the UK. The joy of her dad being on the mend and then the not knowing what to do next.

"Oh, I loved him, and up until then could have sworn he loved me. But there were two reasons why I couldn't just drop everything."

Deb sniggered, and Elle punched her.

"Sorry," Deb said. "Go on. Two reasons?"

"I'd just signed the lease for Chandler's Row and started buying my stock."

"Ah, and the lease was for six months. But he must have known that?"

"Yeah, but his offer was out of the blue, had to start almost immediately, and, well, it was the chance of a lifetime for him. No way could he or should he not go. Talk about timing."

There had been a lot more, but until she, Gus, Angus, and all her family were together, that wasn't for sharing.

"I suggested I could join him then if he was still out there, though I wasn't sure it would be feasible," Elle continued. "He wasn't very happy about it and said he thought if I loved him I'd go like a shot, so we argued, and I did the 'well, if you loved me, you'd understand why I need to stay'. Anyway, off he went, I stayed here, and then Dad got ill and didn't want anyone to know. I only found out because I caught Mum crying. So there was no chance I'd leave when all that was going on. I couldn't tell Gus about Dad, I'd been sworn to secrecy...I only told you cos you sensed something. As it happened, there was no need for me to worry, cos I got a terse wee note saying he was on the move, so don't worry about thinking of giving up my life here." She took a large swig of wine and stared at it as if she had no idea how she came to have it. "Next thing I know is Dad gets the all clear and Gus turns up to say he's back for good."

"With you?"

"Ah, that's the million dollar question isn't it?" Elle said in a cryptic manner. "We hope so."

"Then I can't see a problem," Deb said. "Young, free, and single. Go for it and become young, tied together, and married."

Oh, how to answer that. Her phone saved Elle. It was Gus. "Need to take this," she said to Deb and walked out of the room. Rude perhaps, but even only hearing one side of the conversation, whatever it was going to be, would get Deb asking questions that Elle suspected she wouldn't be able to answer.

"Hi, what's up?"

Gus came straight to the point.

"Said what we decided, but now Dad wants to come and see if you really are all right with everything."

Why on earth hadn't they thought of that earlier? "Good idea, and we could maybe progress to the next part?"

"Certain?" Gus asked. He didn't sound at all worried, so why should she be?

Because I'm not Gus. However, it would be better to get it over and done with.

"Positive. Spill the beans?"

He laughed. "Nope, because I don't abide by any five- or three-second rules. Waste of good beans."

Elle spluttered. Trust him. "You know what I mean."

"Yes, love, of course I do. See you in half an hour or so. I'm cooking, be it for two to four, and Dad needs to nip to the shop on the way."

Elle tapped her phone on her teeth and frowned. Why on earth wasn't life ever simple? She sighed and mentally shook herself as she stared, unseeing, at the clock, and then noticed a cobweb on the wall behind it.

She really was a slob. No time to do anything about it then. She went back to Deb.

"Gus," Elle said, "and I—we—can explain more when he and Angus get here. They'll be half an hour or so."

Deb held up her glass. "Plenty of time for a refill then."

Elle was antsy. What if neither Gus nor Deb understood their actions? Blamed one of them for making the other unhappy? Said they were selfish or…there her mind drew a blank.

She wandered around the kitchen got out plates and glasses and fiddled with the cheese straws, crackers, and dips Deb had put out.

Deb slapped her hands away and removed the plate from within her grasp. "Enough already, stop messing. Anyone would think you were worried or something."

"Ha bloody ha." Elle picked up a wine glass and examined it for smears. The glass sparkled, and tiny rainbows showed in it.

"You dried it, if it's a mess it's your fault." Deb took that from her as well. "Why don't you go and sit down, and oh, I dunno, paint your nails or watch two spiders have a race to see who gets to the top of the wall first."

"Spiders?" Elle gave a yelp. She might be someone who was tolerant of dust bunnies, but spiders were a big no-no. She hadn't seen one near the cobweb, so maybe it was hiding somewhere, ready to scurry out and freak her out. Did spiders in Scotland bite? She'd never thought to check. Maybe that should be the next thing on the agenda.

Or stop being a non-domestic goddess and embrace housework. That was enough to give her the heebie-jeebies as well. Goosebumps ran up her spine. "You've seen spiders? Where?"

"Nowhere, but your fidgeting is beginning to annoy me," Deb replied. "If anyone should be twitchy it should be me. He's a chef, for goodness sake, and I've just got my wee coffee shop. What if he says my dips are runny or my cheese straws not cheesy enough? Or soggy? Ah…now you've got me jittery and worked up."

"He wouldn't be so rude, and if, *if* anyone was so crass, I'd snap at them and say each to their own and how awful if we all liked the same thing." She chose a cheese straw and bit into it. The crunch was satisfactorily loud. "See? Crunchy, though did you say they were supposed to be cheesy?" She ducked the wet dishcloth Deb aimed at her and giggled, suddenly happier. So what if her and Gus' actions weren't to other people's like? They did what they thought was right, and that was that.

The cheese straws, though. She'd better be honest because Deb looked concerned. Elle took another bite. "These are actually delicious," she mumbled through a mouthful of cheesy pastry. "Stop worrying, they are the perfect combination of cheeses and spices. You've got them spot on if you'll take my word for it."

"If you say so." Deb still didn't sound too sure.

"I say so. Now you've nagged me, and I've nagged you, nagging over for now. Drink your wine."

Deb smiled. "Yes, Mum."

Oh lord, she did sound like their mum. Elle had a vision of Melanie Harper, hair in a messy bun, nails painted a deep fuchsia to match her lips, standing in front of them waving a spoon and giving them 'what for'. "Please, not Mum, you'll make me get jittery all over again. Thank goodness they're somewhere near Barbados and not likely to pop in. I couldn't cope with Mum's version of what should be done and she'll not take no for an answer."

"Three weeks and counting," Deb said. "And whatever you think, we have to go to theirs and decorate it for Christmas for them."

Elle groaned. However they decorated, their mum would change it. "I feel some more bah humbug coming on."

"Oh no, you're not allowed to go back to that. After all, what would Gus say?"

"That we've had enough angst at…" She broke off and mimed zipping her lips.

Deb laughed. "You're getting me ever more intrigued," she said as the doorbell rang.

Chapter Ten

In the business of taking coats, asking what Gus and Angus wanted to drink, and under the guise of showing Gus where to put the two large boxes he'd brought with him, Elle got the chance to put one very important question to Gus.

"Is it all okay so far?" God, how needy she sounded. *That's because I am.* "Deb is intrigued, and scared you'll not like her dips and cheese straws."

"Well, I'd rather nibble you," Gus said under his breath then swore as Deb and Angus both wandered into the kitchen. "Those dips look good," he said out loud. "Can I dip and nibble as I cook?"

"Why not, and as it seems we've congregated in here, we might as well talk while you cook." Elle put a cheese straw in his mouth. "Deb can be sous chef."

Deb spluttered, "I'm not good enough to do that. I'll be the underwater ceramic technician."

"Nah, that's Dad's job." Gus took out some wicked-looking knives from one box and indicated the other box with a dip of his head. "If my gorgeous…"

He winked at Elle who went hot and cold.

Not yet, I'm not ready.

"…lady," he went on blithely as if he hadn't noticed her reaction, which she was damned sure he had, "…has a pinny, I'd put it on. Then I'm getting you to do the veg or the veg curry. I'll start the lamb one. Two nights on the trot, but who's counting. This is a treat for Dad, who has been dropping mega hints."

"Cheers." Angus coughed. "But what's what I am?" he asked in a bemused voice. "An underwater what?"

"Dishwasher," Elle said and patted his shoulder. "But we've got a mechanical one to do it, so you're in charge of sorting drinks and some non-Christmas music."

"It is December," he told her. "You always inform me that it starts in December."

Elle rolled her eyes. "Damn."

"That, my love, is what my lovely papa would say is called 'hoist with your own petard." Gus donned the bright-pink pinny Elle handed him. "Not that I know exactly what it means but I reckon it means he's got you there."

"Not if he wants to hear the rest of our story," Elle said. Time to be reckless "I need to concentrate there."

"No Christmas music then," Angus said promptly. "I'll get the drinks and put something soothing on. Start the story."

Elle glanced at Gus, who shrugged. "You've both got the basics, anything else you need to know?"

"I'm happy we've started to understand each other again," Elle said. What more could she add?

"We both know why we did what we did, and hopefully won't need to do anything like it again. Er, what else?"

"Like what happened next?" Deb said.

"We got together, split up because Gus had to go to New Zealand. It was a chance not to be missed, and at the time, I couldn't go with him. He's home, we're going to try again. Be a couple."

Deb sniffed *aww…* "Live together and so on?"

"Of course," Gus said, "wherever Elle wants us to."

Angus cleared his throat. "I'm all for you being a couple but I'm old enough and ornery enough to ask if you're going to make it legal?"

This was it. Elle glanced at Gus who was trying not to laugh. He moved the pans off the Aga, got down on one knee, and cleared his throat.

"Ellie-mine, will you marry me?" The twinkle in his eyes dared her to answer him.

She shrugged and then sighed. "I can't. I'm married already."

"*What*?" Angus and Deb shouted together.

"You never told me that," Deb said reproachfully. "I'm your confidant and I didn't know."

"Wasn't going to share what, after a while, I saw as a mistake."

"But you are married," Deb persisted. "Aren't you?"

Angus stared, and a thoughtful expression crossed his face. "I reckon there's more to this," he said to Deb. "Just you wait."

"Yup." Elle nodded and pointed at the still kneeling Gus. "So is he." She paused. "Married."

Gus got up and gave her a hug before they turned to look at their very interested audience.

Elle chuckled. "He's married to me. Met just before Christmas, married just after Christmas, split at Christmas, and now..." She switched on her iPod where she'd lined up some music.

I Wish it Could Be Christmas Everyday blared out.

Elle laughed at Angus' stunned expression.

"Better than bah humbug."

"Because this Christmas, we're resaying our vows at Christmas. This time in front of family and friends, not over the anvil at Gretna," Gus said with a hint of laughter in his voice. "With the celebrant, two women from a tour bus, three cats, and a kitten."

"This time it's with people who matter."

Printed in Great Britain
by Amazon

53870877R00197